# About the Authors

**Frank Dirscherl** is the author of many novels, including the Amazon bestselling *The Wraith* and *Sanderson of Metro,* as well as several short stories. His *The Wraith Dread Avenger of the Underworld* books have been enjoyed by readers all over the world.

A librarian with over thirty years experience, Frank has also worked at a book wholesaler, a specialist medical practice and as a tutor in the writing and producing of comic books. His interests include reading, traveling, politics, architecture and the environment.

Frank lives in the Illawarra on the south coast of New South Wales, Australia, with his wife and daughter, and is always working on his latest literary endeavors.

**Adam Oravec** is a computer programmer and has been working in the field since 2005. Prior to this he worked in the retail industry. His hobbies include film, theater, writing and reading. He has written one spec script, *The Days of Christopher Robin*, and has contributed Wraith short stories for a variety of anthologies. This is his first novel. He lives in Charlotte, NC USA.

# Praise for *Sanderson of Metro*
## *Amazon* bestseller

"Once shrouded in mystery, The Wraith's stunning origin is finally revealed. Dirscherl and Nash have written one hell of an adventure novel filled with myth, intrigue, and excitement. Highly recommended reading."

– A.P. Fuchs, writer, *The Axiom-man Saga, The Way of the Fog, Undead World trilogy*

"Recommended for Wraith and pulp hero fans."

– Leon Mallett, *Amazon*

"At the end of the day, this novel is a worthy addition to The Wraith's continuing story and a necessary purchase if you're a fan of the character. It's also just a flat out enjoyable reading experience."

– Marcus Bucklin, *Amazon*

"The story is well written, and the Paul Sanderson character fleshed out fairly well...I highly recommend this well written entry for all comic book fans."

– Virginia E. Johnson, *Amazon*

# Praise for *The Wraith*
## *Amazon* bestseller

"I love the coloring job and specially the 'glowing' eyes on the chest of the character."
  - Guillermo del Toro, director, *Blade II, Hellboy I & II*

"I liked the story a lot... It's a very strong debut."
  Steve Englehart, writer, *Detective Comics, The Avengers, Green Lantern*

"I have read the novel (I couldn't put it down)... It is amazing to see how her (Leena) character evolves from Part I to Part II. At first she appears as every other 'girlfriend' in an action film, but those twelve months that pass obviously change her as a person and I love the person she becomes: tougher, but still human."
  - Amber Moelter, actress, *Catwoman: Copycat*

"I finished *The Wraith* book last night. I must say I enjoyed it quite a bit. The scenes kept playing in my head like a big budget Hollywood film. I mentioned earlier that I enjoy when the hero is put to the test physically and doesn't win the battle unscathed. Boy, (Frank) delivered that in spades!"
  - Jeff Welborn, artist, *Nightmare World, The Wraith*

"Genius + sweat + dedication = hard hittin' hero action! Go Aussie!"
  - Dan Lennard, writer, *People* magazine

"*The Wraith* is a wonderful throwback to the purple prose of the bloody pulps with a hero clearly descendant from the likes of the Shadow and the Spider. A fast, action-packed thrill-ride with great characters, both noble and villainous. Slam-bang kick off to a super new series. One I'm anxious to follow."
  – Ron Fortier, writer, *The Spider, Brother Bones, Domino Lady*

"I became familiar with Frank Dirscherl's The Wraith from the comic book of the same name. When the first Wraith novel came out I just had to read it. I was not disappointed. The Wraith is a fast-paced thrill-ride. I'm looking forward to the upcoming sequel."
  – Bobby Nash, writer, *Evil Ways, Fantastix, Lance Star*

"*The Wraith* (is) a really fun read. Have been a fan of Kenneth Robeson's Doc Savage and The Avenger books for years... *The Wraith* reminds me of Robeson at his best."
  – G.R. Lawson, Publisher, General Jinjur Comics

"A short, pulp, superhero novel... Clearly more adventures to come with how this is set up."
  – Richard Scott, *Super Reader* website

"*The Wraith* is an enlightening journey into the darkness of superhero fiction, and a worthy entry into both pulpdom and comicdom."
  – Kevin Noel Olson, *Silver Bullet Comics* website

"*The Wraith* is a testament to Frank's dedication and talent. Other small press characters have come and gone, but The Wraith endures, because Frank understands what makes a classic character."

    – Richard Evans, writer, *The Canadian Legion*

"When it comes to superhero fiction and classic pulp stories, Frank Dirscherl channels those classic adventures of the past into *The Wraith* with ease and gives you a hero to believe in."

    – Stephen J. Semones, writer/director, *Beyond the Lens, Crossfire, The Wraith: Eyes of Judgment*

"Frank Dirscherl's writing is action-packed and reminds me why superhero fiction is so much fun in the first place!"

    – A.P. Fuchs, writer, *The Axiom-man Saga, The Way of the Fog, Undead World trilogy*

"Totally enjoyed this book. Good story, a real hero vs villain yarn. Can't wait to read the other adventures of The Wraith."

    – J. Newey, *Amazon*

# Praise for *Valley of Evil*

"The second Wraith novel is an improvement, I think. Right from the start Dirscherl throws you into the middle of crazy action.... This book is a whole lot of superheroic pulp fun, and the good news is there seems to be more to come...I look forward to some more of the same."
> – Richard Scott, *Super Reader* website

"I think (Dirscherl) really captured a noir element with (his) voice."
> – Joshua Gamon, writer, *Abigail & Rox, Digital Webbing Presents*

"I did quite enjoy the books. Best of all, it wasn't overly sex-filled or gory—I can't stand most modern superhero comics that show such things or have the heroes just swear and swear. So *The Wraith* (and *Valley of Evil*) was just up my alley."
> – Greg Gick, writer, *The Werewolf of Rutherford Grange, Tales of the Shadowmen, Secret Agent X Vol. 2*

"The Dread Avenger is back. After battling the Cobra in his first prose adventure, The Wraith returns to face all new challenges from Metro City's greatest villains, most notably Hong Kong drug kingpin Ma Tzi. As with his first Wraith novel, Frank Dirscherl treats us to a pulp-inspired adventure that keeps readers on the edge of their seat. You have to read this novel in one sitting."
> – Bobby Nash, writer, *Evil Ways, Fantastix, Lance Star*

"In the past five years there has been a tremendous resurgence in pulp fiction centering on the old heroic pulps. Young writers have started taking up the mantle of old masters like Walter Gibson and Lester Dent and begun creating their own avengers in tales of genuine purple prose. Among the best of this new generation of wordsmiths is Australian, Frank Dirscherl and the exploits of his modern pulp paladin, The Wraith. This is grand pulp!"

   –  Ron Fortier, writer, *The Spider, Brother Bones, Domino Lady*

# Praise for *Crossfire*

"Stephen did a fantastic job of bringing Frank Dirscherl's character to life!"
  - Adam DiTroia, composer, *The Wraith: Eyes of Judgment*, MTV, Fox Sports

"Loved the book!! Can't wait for the next installment..."
  - Larry Mainland, actor, *The Walking Dead, Lawless, The Three Stooges*

"The action comes swift, and doesn't stop until the final pages. *Crossfire* tells a great story of betrayal and revenge."
  - C.R. Blevins, writer, *A Western Tale*

"This was my first introduction to The Wraith and I was not disappointed. The action comes swift, and doesn't stop until the final pages.... If you love a good action/hero story, you will certainly enjoy reading *Crossfire*."
  - Ally, *Amazon*

"Makes me want more...should be the next series on Netflix..."
  - Bill Lancaster, *Amazon*

"Another excellent entry in The Wraith Adventures series. Thoroughly recommended for Wraith fans and fans of pulp super-heroics."
  - Leon Mallett, *Amazon*

# Praise for *Cult of the Damned*

"Only by the first three pages, Frank Dirscherl wonderfully captures a dark and mysterious atmosphere, one that leaves the reader with a cryptic and eerie sensation; one that makes me cold just thinking about it."

> – Rennie Cowan, writer/director, *The Thriller Idol: A Tribute to the Legacy of Michael Jackson, Kade the Conqueror*

"Frank Dirscherl pulls you into the world of The Wraith from the first sentence and refuses to let you go until the last one."

> – Stephen J. Semones, writer/director, *Beyond the Lens, Crossfire, The Wraith: Eyes of Judgment*

"The Wraith is one of my favorite characters and every time Frank Dirscherl puts pen to paper I know I'm in for a real treat."

> – A.P. Fuchs, writer, *The Axiom-man Saga, The Way of the Fog, Undead World trilogy*

# Praise for *Cry of the Werewolf*

"Frank Dirscherl delivers beyond measure.... The solid characters, settings and story really propel you page to page and leave you hanging on for more."
- Stephen J. Semones, writer/director, *Beyond the Lens, Crossfire, The Wraith: Eyes of Judgment*

"Each new installment in *The Wraith Adventures* series is a guaranteed good time filled with high adventure, romance and pulpy fun. Dirscherl is at the top of his form."
- A.P. Fuchs, writer, *The Axiom-man Saga, The Way of the Fog, Undead World trilogy*

"The writing is well done and well edited, and is filled with that distinct Dirscherl style of pulp that I enjoy so much. The book is a perfect example of what Neo Pulp/Superhero and Horror fiction can be and is a worthy addition to any fan's collection."
- Marcus Bucklin, *Amazon*

# Praise for *Vendetta*

"...in all a great brew that had me hooked for the whole ride. Now bring on the next book, Frank..."

– Leon Mallett, Amazon

"This book starts with a literal bang and doesn't let the foot off of the gas until the very last page. The book is well plotted and moves at a breakneck pace, making it an enjoyable, short read. I loved this book very much as a fan of The Wraith and I believe that anyone who is a fan of the series should consider this required reading."

– Marcus Bucklin, Amazon

# Praise for *Zombies Attack!* in *Metahumans vs the Undead*

"This compilation of superheroes vs evil offers top entertainment for superhero lovers! Frank Dirscherl and others are at their best with their contributed stories. I will now pursue other stories written by these authors, such as those involving Mr. Dirscherl's The Wraith. This type of reading enjoyment knows no end!"

– 　　Ramona Wingart, writer, *Where is Brother Beaver?*, *Emily Suzanne Smith!*

## Praise for *Werewolves Attack!* in *Metahumans vs Werewolves*

"Always a great read. Can never put it down once you get started... "

– Geraldine L. Lewis, *Amazon*

# BY FRANK DIRSCHERL

## FICTION

*The Wraith Dread Avenger of the Underworld* series

*Sanderson of Metro* (with Bobby Nash)
*Serpent Rising* (with Greg Gick)
*The Wraith*
*Valley of Evil*
*Crossfire* (with Stephen J. Semones)
*Cult of the Damned*
*Cry of the Werewolf*
*Swamp Witch of Satan's Forest* (with Ray MacKay)
*Vendetta*
*Lady Wraith* (with Adam Oravec)
*Kingdom* - COMING SOON
*City of Fear* - COMING SOON

## SHORT STORY COLLECTIONS

*Metahumans vs. the Undead*
*Metahumans vs. Werewolves*
*Metahumans vs. Robots*
*Metahumans vs. the Ultimate Evil*
*Lance Star – Sky Ranger Vol. 1*
*The Wraith Vol. 1*

## NON-FICTION

*The Wraith: Eyes of Judgment – The Official Script Book & Movie Guide*
(with Stephen J. Semones)
*The Hitchers of Oz*
*Beyond the Lens* (edited)

**www.glowingeyesmedia.com**

# LADY WRAITH

The Wraith Dread Avenger of the Underworld #8

by

Frank Dirscherl & Adam Oravec

GLOWING EYES MEDIA

WOLLONGONG

GLOWING EYES MEDIA
PO Box 31
Wollongong NSW 2520

ISBN 978-0-6457475-7-7

LADY WRAITH

PUBLISHED BY GLOWING EYES MEDIA, April 2025
www.glowingeyesmedia.com
FRONT COVERT ART by Gregory Price & Anon
COVER LAYOUT AND DESIGN AND INTERIOR DESIGN by Frank Dirscherl
EDITED by AP Fuchs
FIRST EDITION

For more on *Lady Wraith*
visit www.glowingeyesmedia.com

Text set in Garamond-Normal. Printed and bound in the USA

NATIONAL
LIBRARY
OF AUSTRALIA
A catalogue record for this book is available from the National Library of Australia

*The Wraith Dread Avenger of the Underworld* series
in correct reading order (including short stories)

**So far...but the story goes on...**

# LADY WRAITH

# ~ Prologue ~

A FEW WEEKS EARLIER

"**H**urry up, idiots! Get that crap on board!"

The Wraith watched on from his high vantage point as a burly man, stocky of build with a face akin to a granite slab, shouted to his gang, a series of seedy-looking thugs removing crates from a small, decrepit vessel docked in the long-abandoned Christopher Docks in Metro's Eastside. They lugged them up the lengthy wharf as efficiently as possible toward a series of small trucks parked alongside a derelict warehouse.

"We're moving as fast as we can," one thug moaned. "These bloody things are heavy."

"Cut the lip!" the burly man fired off. "We ain't got all night!"

"All right, all right," the thug moaned. "What is this we're hauling, anyway?"

The burly man, his face contorted in a tight grimace, removed a gun from a holster contained within his black coat and aimed it at the questioning thug. He fired without saying a word.

"Anyone else have anything cute to say? No? Then keep moving!"

The rest of the gang, briefly shocked at the murder of their comrade, nevertheless acquiesced and picked up the pace. Their former friend lay in a pool of blood as they passed by him time and again with their cargo.

The burly man, tall and built like a wardrobe, wore a tight-fitting albeit quality Italian suit and stood guard over the others with a lecherous grin. He clearly reveled in the power he had. Or thought he had. The Wraith knew it was time to make him see the error of his ways.

Minutes dragged on into hours before all the trucks were finally filled with their cargo of wooden crate after crate.

"That's it, boys, knock-off time," the burly man shouted. "You'll be paid at the usual time and place. Now get outta here!"

Before the group could disperse, a gas pellet was lobbed into the center of them, enveloping them in a thick, pungent haze.

"What the–" the burly guard yelled.

Panic rose amongst the others as they cried out and darted here and there, not knowing where to go or what to do.

The Dread Avenger dropped down and lunged into the melée, lashing out with fists and feet at everyone in his path. Wearing his re-breather and night-vision lenses, he made easy work of the entire bunch of around twenty men. As the smoke began to dissipate, one man remained to face The Wraith.

"Y...you," the burly man coughed. "We...we was told you were...were..."

"Were what?" The Wraith replied. "Tell me!"

The burly man prepared himself for a fight, legs akimbo, fists raised. "Doesn't matter. I can take you. Ain't lost a fight yet, especially to a runt like you."

The Wraith smiled. These muscular himbos always felt superior in every way. Despite his recent exhaustion, having only just vanquished Crossfire a mere week earlier after his arch-nemesis had nearly destroyed the entire city, he almost relished the lesson he was about to impart on his rugged opponent. "Then come forth. Judgment is waiting for you."

The burly man snarled and lunged at the Dread Avenger in an attempt to grapple him into a wrestling hold. The Wraith saw the maneuver coming a mile away and quickly sidestepped his adversary, lashing out with a karate chop to the back of the neck.

The burly man fell to his knees but was otherwise unharmed. "You a quick little guy, ain't ya." The fact The Wraith was several inches taller clearly made little difference to the thug. He gnashed his teeth and went on the attack again, swinging with a right and a left, neither connecting. "Stand still and fight, will ya?"

Taking the offensive, the Eyes of Judgment on his chest burst into electrical life, strobing an almost sickening yellow hue. He advanced upon his prey, the burly man inching backwards, fear etched into his features. "You who would inflict misery on others. You who would bring pain and death into my city...now face true justice. Judgment!"

As the burly man crashed backwards onto his rear, The Wraith sallied forth to inflict his Judgment Stare on the hapless thug. Then, a creaking sound came from behind him. The Wraith whirled and blackness enveloped him, body and soul.

# ~ Chapter 1 ~

THE PRESENT

*T*he *search, this long, tormenting search. Will there ever be an end to it?*

Leena Patterson, The Wraith's partner in life and in his war on crime, sat in near darkness within The Wraith's Lair, their stronghold located within the center of the great Sanderson House mansion where she and the love of her life, Paul Sanderson aka The Wraith, lived together in the heart of Metro City. She shook her thoughts away and returned to the job at hand, tapping away at the great computer terminal situated within the center of the Lair. The Wraith had gone missing five weeks earlier while out on patrol. Neither she nor their right-hand man Max Horton could raise him on radio. It was as though he had just vanished into thin air. No evidence, no apparent witnesses. No leads of any kind to go on. So, in her new guise as Lady Wraith, she had spent the last five weeks patrolling the city, hitting the city's informants, drug pushers, pimps and hookers hard. She left no stone unturned in her unrelenting search.

Nothing came of her investigation until word arose a particularly nasty snitch and jerk-of-all trades, new to the city and known colloquially as Fatback, may have some information about an incident at the Christopher Docks around the time of The Wraith's disappearance. His location had thus far been impossible to ascertain, but a method of communication–achieved through much violence–had been discovered. A burner phone lay before Leena on the desk. It was just a matter of waiting.

Impatiently, she turned in her chair and came face-to-face with Max Horton, who was working nearby on some equipment within the Lair's tech lab. He eyed her sympathetically but said nothing. He knew what was at stake. He knew the turmoil she was going through. She returned his glance with one of her own.

The burner phone rang, briefly startling her. She spun back around quickly and answered, putting the phone on speaker. "That you, Fatty?"

Fatback's cranky voice boomed out of the phone. "Don't call me that!" A brief pause. "Who is this? How did you get this number?"

"You know who this is. I'm sure your friends–those that can still talk–must have told you all about me."

Another pause, a silence Leena found unbearable. "Lady Wraith," Fatback said with a sleazy glee. "I've heard of you. Whatever could you want with me?"

"Word is, you know something..."

"I know a lot of things," Fatback grunted, interrupting.

"...about an incident on the Christopher Docks a few weeks ago."

Another silent pause. This must be Fatback's stock-in-trade. Clearly he's a master at annoying people. "I might. I just might. But...we need to meet. I don't want to talk about it on the phone. I'll be in touch."

Before Leena could argue, he hung up. Leena slammed her fist into the desk in anger and frustration, causing the phone to career onto the floor. Was this another dead end? Was Fatback merely stringing her along or did he actually know something of value? At this point, she could only wait, and hope for the best.

\* \* \* \* \* \* \*

Detective Bob Sloan stood next to a uniformed police officer, as the officer pointed toward the opposite end of the street. Police lights, shimmering blue and white, bounced off snowflakes to illuminate the cordoned-off stretch of road. Sloan raised his arm to shield his eyes.

"We got here quickly, sir," the police officer said. "Ain't nothing getting through. We told the media this was a drill."

"Hell," Sloan grunted, "I didn't want the media to know about this at all just yet. Now they're guaranteed to show up in force. They're not gonna buy that drill story."

He rubbed his hands together in an attempt to ward off the cold. He'd forgotten his gloves again. The adrenalin of another case was coursing through him, but even that wasn't enough to shield his aging bones from the inclement weather. As several officers lingered around him, he missed his partner Rosa Perez evermore. She had recently taken a leave of absence, the mysterious depression afflicting half the city having finally taken its toll on her, and she had decided to take some well-deserved leave, visiting with friends interstate. While Sloan was glad she had finally taken some action to address her state of mind, he missed her all the same. Nobody had his back like she did.

After a moment, he turned to the officer nearest him. "Okay, we haven't got all night. Let's view the crime scene."

Several officers brushed past Sloan, rushing toward the building in question. Before Sloan could move more than a few steps in their direction, a familiar sound greeted his ears. It was down the street, by the nearest cordon, but he recognized it instantly. And dreaded it.

"Crap!"

\* \* \* \* \* \* \*

Two news vans were parked right beside the barricades with various cameramen and technicians already appearing ready to run the police gauntlet. Gayle Rodgers of *News Media Ten*, perfectly outfitted and coiffured, was the last to exit. She brushed the creases from her cream blouse, reached up to check her hair was in its proper place, then turned to a colleague. "My makeup okay?"

"Sure, why wouldn't it be?" the colleague replied indifferently.

"Are you available for comment, Officer...?" Rodgers asked, practically knocking the barricade over while doing so.

"Hey, hey," the officer shouted. "Nobody gets in here."

"Look, we just want a comment. What's happened here? Can we get you on record, on camera?"

"Rodgers," Sloan said as he moved alongside the officer manning the barricade, "we have no comment to give *News Media Ten* at this time."

"Your disdain for us," Rodgers said sharply, "is so blatantly obvious." She smoothed the creases from her trousers.

"You guys make *Fox News* look like paragons of truth and justice," Sloan grunted.

"I'm just doing my job," Rodgers said, puffing out her chest. Her pride had been dented.

"So am I," Sloan said. "Officer, make sure these people *do not* cross this line. It's your head if they do."

"Yessir," he replied, saluting.

"But, Detective Sloan," Rodgers cried out.

Sloan started to make his way down the street but stopped and turned to face the journalist. "You'll get a statement of the facts–and only the bare facts–when I am ready to give one...*not* before."

With that, he turned and left.

# ~ Chapter 2 ~

Sloan stood at the ground floor apartment's doorway, surveying the interior. It was a typical rundown tenement, sparsely furnished, disgustingly filthy, and stinking of goodness knows what. Sloan quickly pulled out a handkerchief and placed it over his face. He now recognized the stench of decaying flesh.

CSI technicians, outfitted in protective gear, marched here and there. Gloved officers manned the various entrances. Flashes from cameras lit up the gloom.

"Looks like this place hasn't been lived in for a while," one young officer said to Sloan.

Sloan looked him over. New to the force, he thought. Still green and fresh. He didn't know if this was a good or bad thing. "Where's the body?"

"Body?" the young officer said, raising an eyebrow. "Oh, the smell. It's just a couple of dead dogs over there." He pointed to a spot behind the sofa.

"Then why are we here? Who called this in?"

"A neighbor, a Mrs...Smith," the young officer said, referring to a small notebook, "said there have been so many loud comings and goings the last day or two, caused such a commotion, that she had to call the police."

Sloan rolled his eyes. "That's all? Come on." He gripped the bridge of his nose.

"I think you'll find there's a great deal to see here," the young officer reported. "Through there." He pointed.

Sloan sighed, prepared to head in the direction indicated. "Anyone else see anything worth noting?"

"We're canvasing the area now. Should have something soon."

Sloan, pulling on rubber gloves, inched his way through the living room. He did his best to avoid the rodent droppings scattered throughout the similarly-colored threadbare carpet. The faux leather sofa was cracked and scattered with what appeared to be mold.

At the far end of the living room by the entrance to the kitchen the wall was streaked with a dry, brown liquid. Technicians were attempting to collect samples of it as Sloan passed and made his way slowly into the kitchen.

The grey linoleum was faded and peeling. The kitchen counters were in the same, ugly hue. The sink was cracked and stained, food-stained dishes and utensils, covered with ants and cockroaches, were scattered within.

Beyond the kitchen lay a dingy, narrow hallway. As Sloan entered, he saw two closed doors facing him at the opposite end. A uniformed officer stood sentinel there.

"Detective Sloan, sir?" the officer said.

Sloan nodded.

"You're wanted down this way, in the basement." He indicated the door on his right.

Sloan looked at him.

*A basement in an apartment? Oh-kay...*

He opened the door and made his way slowly down the rickety staircase. Lights were extant at the bottom. He removed the handkerchief, the smell having faded with the distance.

Reaching bottom, Sloan saw several more technicians and detectives surveying the scene. In the center of all the activity was a detective Sloan knew well–and disliked just as much– Robert Anderson. A contemporary of Sloan, but much thinner and with less hair, Anderson saw himself as something of a rival to his colleague. Indeed, he saw himself as the next Commissioner of Police. In truth, Anderson was a well-dressed specimen, preferring Italian suits to American, but he was arrogant and oftentimes painfully ignorant. Nevertheless, perhaps surprisingly, he made for a passable cop. And he wasn't dirty. How he managed to reach the scene first, Sloan could only guess. Anderson and a CSI technician were making a careful examination of a wooden strut, one of several within the basement. On the post in question, there were several scratch marks in the wood as well as indentations near the bottom. Anderson rubbed his head.

"What have we got here?" Sloan asked as nobody seemed to as yet have noticed his presence.

"Sloan," Anderson said, displaying some surprise. "What are you doing here? This is my case."

"There's no ownership on cases in Metro, you know that, Anderson," Sloan said. "We work together on this, as always."

Anderson muttered something under his breath but said nothing else.

The CSI technician beside Anderson took the initiative. "You see these indentations at the bottom?"

Sloan nodded.

"These aren't scratches, not really," the technician said, crouched while pointing at the marks. "They're bite marks."

Sloan's eyes opened wide in surprise and stared at the technician. "An animal's? We have dead dogs upstairs."

"No, no," the technician said. "The size and shape are all wrong."

The realization of whose they must be shocked even an experienced investigator like Sloan. The marks were human. What in God's name happened here?

The technician stood and motioned to the scratches above the bite marks. She wrapped her arms around the post. "Visualize this...my arms are here, shackled. The chains are grinding against the wood." The technician bent to a spot lower down, just above the bite marks "Then here, more grinding, then finally biting."

"Good God," Sloan whispered. The horror of it all was beginning to dawn on him. After a moment, he collected his thoughts. "So this was a shorter person, judging by the height of these marks."

The technician gravely nodded. "The size of the bite marks don't support that."

Sloan gasped. "A child..." he said softly.

The technician nodded. Sloan stared grimly at Anderson, then back at the technician. All were cognizant of the depravity of the situation, albeit completely in the dark as to the whys and hows.

"And over here," the technician continued, walking over to another post, "grinding, just like the first."

Sloan rubbed his chin, tried to make sense of the senseless. "So, we have two people–children–here? Chained like animals?"

"At least," the technician replied. "We're still checking for any other indications." She took a step back, pointed higher up the post. "There's more."

Sloan craned his vision to the exact spot indicated. His sight was no longer the best. He probably needed glasses though he was resistant to admitting it. "What is that?"

"Something carved," Anderson broke in. "Initials."

"A P and an S," the technician said.

Sloan scratched his head, not knowing what to make of all this. "Is there any way to determine the age of those marks, these carvings? Even to my aging eyes, they look pretty fresh."

"Very fresh," the technician said. "At a guess, I'd say a few weeks, no more. They all appear to be of the same vintage."

Sloan rubbed his chin. "A child," he whispered again. He moved over to the carved initials. They were higher than any child could reach. "This is clearly an adult's doing."

"Or a tall teen," Anderson said sharply.

Sloan looked at him but said nothing.

"We find this P.S., we crack this whole thing wide open," Anderson said.

Sloan rolled his eyes. If only it was that simple. But, yes, potentially linking those initials with that address might prove useful. Then again, knowing the likelihood of what had occurred here–some sort of kidnapping, perhaps connected with sex slavery or child pornography–meant the chances of linking the two were very slim.

"I want this place combed for clues," Sloan said at last. "Take it apart if you have to. There has to be something more here. Prints, hair, fingernails–something! Who owns this apartment? Did they live here? Was it leased out? I want everything there is to know about this place and the people who lived or stayed here."

"What do you think we've been doing?" Anderson fired back. "You're not talking to some junior constable, you know."

"Yes, sir," the technician said to Sloan. She appeared eager to please.

Sloan looked to Anderson and motioned for the two of them to head upstairs. Anderson, frowning, nevertheless acquiesced.

"What the hell is this all about, Sloan?" Anderson was clearly fumed upon reaching the darkened hallway upstairs. "I told you this was my case."

"I'm the senior detective here," Sloan said firmly. "You know that as well as I do. Enough of this ownership crap. We work together. We're a team whether you like it or not." He hated having to deal with this sort of garbage.

Anderson stood archly but remained silent. His demeanor, his facial expression, spoke volumes.

"We do this by the book, and we do this right. No stone unturned. We find out what the hell happened here no matter what."

Anderson seemed to calm down at this. His professionalism, whatever that was worth, began to work on his nerves. "The Gosch case," he said finally.

"What?"

"The Gosch case," Anderson repeated. "Don't you remember? Epstein's delivery men. This appears to have some similarities."

Sloan thought and remembered. Perhaps Anderson was right. It was certainly worth looking into either way.

"Good work. Get on it."

Anderson smiled ever so slightly but clearly was trying to hide it.

Sloan turned and began to make his way back through the abode toward the front door.

\* \* \* \* \* \* \*

Lady Wraith, her suit almost identical to The Wraith's, stood atop a city rooftop, the darkness of the night enveloping her. The bitterly cold winter wind snaked its way around her body. Even outfitted in her protective suit, she swore she could feel a chill in her very bones. She took a deep breath, feeling a sting in her nostrils. She closed her eyes. Memories of her life with Paul flooded her consciousness. Paul had vanished once before, back when he was known as Michael Reeve, the police constable she had fallen in love with all those years ago. But he returned, and upon his return, her life had changed forever. Now calling himself Paul Sanderson, he had also revealed himself to be The Wraith, the Dread Avenger of the Underworld that Michael had long revered. Now he was gone again. But this was worse. Far, far worse. What on Earth was she doing there?

All she wanted to do was get out there and find Paul, find out what happened to him. But, as Max had reminded her, her best course of action was to wait to hear from Fatback, and until that time, crime in Metro would not take a backward step. She needed to do as much as possible to help the war on crime in Paul's absence, and, perhaps, the exertion would help take her mind off her tribulations. But she knew better. Nothing could make her forget the love of her life.

She tried to shake all that from her mind, moved over to the edge of the building, gravel crunching underfoot. From her current vantage point, Metro City looked stunning, the city lights powerfully beaming through the snow, which had only just begun to fall, glistening like a tremendous Christmas tree. It was only at ground level the city's true nature became plainly visible.

She heard a crackle in her earpiece. It was Max on the comm-link. Her heart skipped a beat. Could it be word on Paul? "Yes, Max?"

"How are you holding up?" Max said, trying to sound upbeat, but she knew then there would be no new information forthcoming, and her spirit sank.

"I'm fine. Patrol is proceeding on schedule. Nothing untoward so..."

Lady Wraith stopped in her tracks. She heard grinding metal-on-metal in the alleyway below. She peered downward, touched at her temple. Lenses dropped down in place over her eyes within her cowl. Night-vision and telescopic, she could see the below scene in all its seedy glory.

Several members of the Vice Lords gang were attempting to break into a large, metal door in the adjacent building. Thus far, they weren't making the best job of it and creating a bit of a ruckus in doing so.

"Max, I'll get back to you. I've spotted some trouble."

Switching her lenses and comm-link off, she readied herself for action.

# ~ Chapter 3 ~

"Come on, we don't have all day," one of the gang members, evidently the leader of the bunch, sternly said.

"I'm going as fast as I can," came the angry whispered reply from the one attempting to use a crowbar on the jewelry store rear entrance.

The leader leaned impatiently against the building wall while two others paced nearby. All were outfitted in the trademark garb of the Vice Lords: Leather jackets with their logo, a skull with two large daggers protruding from the eye holes, emblazoned on the rear. The leader appeared the tallest, and burliest, of the group, with a loud hairdo to match his voice.

Finally, an earsplitting crack was heard and the door opened slowly.

"About bloody time," the leader roared. "And we coulda done without the racket."

"Ease up, will ya?"

Before another word could be spoken, the leader went flying, smashing into the adjacent wall with a thud. He fell to his knees in front of his comrades. They all turned to face Lady Wraith, her fury evident in the fear on their faces.

"Evildoers," she bellowed in a voice not too dissimilar to that of The Wraith himself, "your time of judgment is at hand."

The leader struggled to his feet, the wind having been knocked out of him. He eyed Lady Wraith carefully, recognition dawning upon his face. "This ain't The Wraith," he said, relief evident in his voice. "This is just some silly girl playing dress-up."

"I don't know," a third gang member spoke. "I hearda this *Lady Wraith*. She ain't no pushover."

"You gonna let a dame push us around?" the leader fired back. "Man up. Get her. Show this chick the Vice Lords don't take no orders from any woman."

The three gang members charged Lady Wraith in unison. A spinning side kick sent all three to the ground. One was up quickly, swung at her with the crowbar. He managed to graze her arm with the swing, but no more. She circled her right arm around, grabbed his underneath and twisted. He screamed in agony as bone snapped and the crowbar crashed to the ground. She followed with a left to the face. Down he went.

The other two faced her, front and back. She kicked one in the stomach, doubling him over, then swiveled and punched the other in the nose. She turned back to the first and kneed him in the face. He went sprawling into the pavement.

Two left. The leader finally entered the fray, grunted as he leaped forward, trying to use his muscle against his much leaner adversary. It was no good. Muscular he may have been, but skilled in hand-to-hand combat he was not. Lady Wraith lashed out with blows to the face and abdomen in quick succession. The fury of the assault seemed to cause the remaining gang member to think better of the struggle. He turned and ran.

Lady Wraith raised her arm and aimed her grapnel, fired, the line catching the thug by the ankle. He careened face first into the sidewalk. She yanked back on the line, drawing the hapless Vice Lord back toward her. Turning around, he looked up at Lady Wraith...and screamed.

"Judgment is upon you," she said as the Eyes of Judgment on her chest burst to life.

\* \* \* \* \* \* \*

Sloan sat alone at his desk at Metro Police Plaza, ruminating over a slew of paperwork. His partner Rosa Perez's desk across from him was both tidy and deserted. Neither were normal occurrences. Truth be told, he felt a little lost without his partner. Not only was she a great cop, someone that had his back like no other, but she was also the best friend he had ever known. He could only hope, wherever she was, whatever she was doing, she was getting the help that she needed.

Sloan hunched over his desk and briefly looked again at the reams in front of him. It was hard to keep his mind on them, not after what he had just seen. People being kept prisoner, some of them children. A seasoned cop, a cop who had seen pretty much everything a cesspool like Metro could throw at him– nevertheless, the picture that apartment had etched into his mind sickened him. He was determined to get some answers.

"There's someone here to see you, Sloan," a uniformed officer called out from the far end of the station.

He lifted an eyebrow. At this hour?

"Who is it?"

"Anderson sent for him, from a precinct across town. He worked the Johnny Gosch case apparently."

*That was quick*, Sloan thought. *Anderson doesn't waste any time. Good.*

"Show him up," Sloan said. He pushed the paperwork to one side. They could wait; he had more important things to deal with.

A few moments later, a tall, muscular, middle-aged man strode forcefully toward Sloan. Sloan stood to greet him. He had a full head of bleach-blond hair, and a forceful shake upon taking Sloan's outstretched hand.

"Detective Bob Sloan. Thanks for coming in so quickly."

"Opperman," came the reply. "Sean. A Detective Anderson called me in, said you wanted some help since I worked the Gosch case."

Help may have been a strong word, but yes, any input this Opperman could supply would be most welcome.

"Yes, so I'm told."

Sloan indicated Opperman take a seat in Perez's chair.

"So, what can I do to help?" Opperman said.

Sloan took the next few minutes to update him on the crime scene he had just witnessed only a short time earlier. He described the scene in great detail, leaving nothing out. Opperman sat silently and stoically, seemingly taking it all in. After Sloan finished, Opperman sat silently for a few more moments, then sat upright in his chair.

"Yes, there are some similarities to the Gosch case," Opperman said at last. He shifted in his chair. "Johnny

Gosch, snatched from his home as a child. Years later, now almost fully grown, he shows up at his parents' house. He had managed to escape the nightmare he had been caught up in, but he was damaged almost beyond repair." Opperman breathed heavily. It was evident to Sloan that just repeating this story was taking a toll on his fellow cop.

"Go on," Sloan said.

"It was nearly a year before Gosch was able to speak, able to tell us the hell he had been through."

"Child pornography?"

"Pedophile ring...on a massive scale," Opperman whispered, apparently almost unwilling to speak the words aloud.

Sloan rubbed his chin. He hadn't worked that case; it had been out of his jurisdiction, and it had been years earlier, but the memory of it was coming back to him. What he remembered of it appalled him.

"With Gosch's help, we were able to round up many of those responsible. Many of whom were linked to Jeffrey Epstein," Opperman continued. "And just like Epstein, many of those ended up committing *suicide.*" Opperman made quotation marks with his fingers for that last word.

"There's no proof Epstein was murdered," Sloan said sharply, "and I don't recall there being any proof in the Gosch case either."

"Cover up," Opperman said quietly and matter-of-factly. He leaned back in his chair and said nothing more.

Sloan shook his head. "Oh no. You're not one of these conspiracy nuts, are you? If so, you're of no help to me whatsoever. I don't think we should even continue–"

Opperman leaned forward again, appeared somewhat angry, but did not raise his voice. "Of course, we couldn't prove it. There'll *never* be proof. The feds took care of that and always will."

Sloan raised his eyebrows. "Do you realize what you're saying? The feds are running some sex trafficking enterprise?"

"Not running it, no. But protecting many of those who...utilize its services, shall we say, yes."

Sloan didn't know what to think, what to believe.

"And no, I'm not some nut, as you put it," Opperman went on. "Security footage magically disappeared, files were deleted or went missing, witnesses suddenly refused to testify....You name it, we came up against all of it. We had just enough left to convict some of the little guys, those personally responsible for snatching and imprisoning Gosch, but the bigger fry, the abusers, the ringleaders...all got away Scot-free."

Sloan scratched his head.

"Trust me, it's politicians, it's city officials throughout the country, DAs, church officials...even cops. But there's no evidence. Nothing!"

Sloan softly whistled. He hated to believe it, but he knew deep down Opperman was on the level. This was big. Hell, big was an understatement. Finally, he said, "So, if this new case is similar, maybe even connected somehow to the Gosch case...how do we end up with a different resolution? How do we nail these bastards to the wall?"

Opperman leaned forward in his chair once more. "We work together on this, hand-in-glove. All the detailed work we keep to ourselves but a small handful of those we trust. And maybe, just maybe...we can get somewhere."

Sloan pondered this. He was potentially getting in deep, deeper than anything he'd been involved with before. The consequences, for him, for his family and loved ones, were monumental. But these scumbags had to pay. If he took this on–which was now a foregone conclusion–he needed help. *They* needed help. The kind of help that Opperman would have no comprehension of.

The Wraith.

"Okay," he said under his breath even though there were few other cops within earshot at such a late hour, "first we find out who owned and-or leased today's crime scene. That might lead us somewhere."

"Maybe," Opperman said, "but most likely up a blind alley. They're too clever to be discovered that easily. They'll be using false names, dummy corporations, that sort of thing."

"Even so," Sloan said, "we have to start somewhere. Look...I'll put in the paperwork for your transfer here. Make up some story or other to explain it all. Then we get cracking, get our *covert* team together."

Opperman stood, nodded his understanding. "Agreed. I'll get prepared, then." He turned to leave.

"Opperman," Sloan called out. "If this is as you say...watch your back."

"Don't worry, I have been. I will."

He exited, leaving Sloan alone with his thoughts.

\* \* \* \* \* \* \*

Now snowing steadily, Lady Wraith continued her nightly patrol, breaking up another attempted burglary, a few muggings, and a potential rape. All-in-all a successful night. But her thoughts were always on Paul, his whereabouts, his safety. It was not knowing that hurt the most. He may even be dead...

*No,* she thought. *If Paul is dead, I would feel it somehow, I just know it. No, I have to continue on the basis he's alive, somehow, somewhere...*

Running across a rooftop, her comm link suddenly crackled to life. "Yes, Max?"

"Fatback wants to meet. Tonight."

"Where?"

\* \* \* \* \* \* \*

The snow cover was building up fast, especially in the secluded alley where Fatback slowly paced, rubbing his hands together in a vain attempt to keep them warm.

*Must be minus twenty-five out here. What was I thinking? If she's not here in another couple minutes, screw her!*

"Fatty," a voice emanated from the shadows.

He jumped, caught completely off guard. Lady Wraith slinked into the low light in front of him. He couldn't help but take a backward step or three.

"What the hell, woman! And don't call me that!"

"Where is he?" she said, ignoring his outrage. "Where is The Wraith?"

Fatback held up both hands in mock surrender. "I ain't got nothin' on that."

She growled and began advancing toward him. He retreated again.

"Hang on, hang on," he said, trying to halt her progress. "There's this place, near Main Street. The cops raided it yesterday. A trap house...for kids."

Lady Wraith lost her patience, grabbed Fatback by the collar, and slammed him into the adjacent wall. "What does this have to do with The Wraith?"

"It wa...wasn't j...just a trap house," Fatback said. "They were involved with drugs, weapons imports, other crap. All came through the abandoned Christopher Docks."

"So?"

"So," he started, Lady Wraith having loosened her grip somewhat, "a guy I know did drugs in that apartment. He was there when...*mighta* been there when...your guy was there..."

She grabbed him good and tight again and shook him hard.

"Hey, hey, he's a druggie, he could be blowing steam. Then again, he could be legit. I can't say. But it's all I have." He then related the man's address to her.

Lady Wraith threw him aside. Thankfully, it was a deep snowdrift that caught his sizable carcass.

"I don't have time to chase geese," Lady Wraith said firmly. "If I find out this is bull...you better be in hiding because I will come for you!"

She stood there, making sure he understood the menace in his stare. He believed her. What had he gotten himself into here? Was all this worth it? Then, he thought again of the trap house. The kids.

"I done some messed up stuff in my life," Fatback said, his words seeming to follow his thoughts as he tried to stagger to his feet, "but I ain't never touched kids. That's a whole 'nother level of sick."

Fatback finally managed to get himself up through the snow, raised his head to face Lady Wraith. But she was nowhere to be seen. The night had swallowed her up as quickly as it had spat her out. He tried to brush away the snow from his clothes. Man it was cold. He looked up again where Lady Wraith had been standing.

"You're welcome."

\* \* \* \* \* \* \*

Anderson sat at his desk, attempting to write an initial report on the crime scene for Commissioner Harrison, when Sloan sauntered up to him.

"You got a minute?" Sloan asked.

Anderson stopped typing, sighed. He hated being interrupted when he was in the middle of something, anything. Was one of his pet peeves. "Yes?" he huffed.

Sloan crouched beside him and spoke in a hushed tone. "Look, this case...I think you were on the money with the link to the Gosch case."

"Opperman been in touch, then?"

"He has," Sloan said, "and we had a long chat earlier. This could be big...real big. And I want–need–you in on this. I know we've...clashed from time-to-time in the past, but...there aren't many here I trust. And we–the three of us–need to surround ourselves with as few people, trustworthy people, that we can muster. Unofficially, that is."

Anderson's ears perked up at this. It all sounded rather clandestine, but, he liked the thought of it. Plus, this case could really make his name in the force, could thrust him upwards into the Commissioner's office, or even beyond. He couldn't say no.

"Look, officially, we handle this case as we always would, but if word comes from above to stop, or sidestep, we do it. Then go underground with our investigation. Understand?"

Anderson nodded.

"I'll arrange a meeting for the three of us soon, plan our next step. Until then, we go on as normal, until or unless we're forced to do otherwise."

Anderson again nodded.

"Okay, good. I'm counting on you." Sloan retreated, leaving Anderson with a lot to think about.

\* \* \* \* \* \* \*

Sloan stood atop the Metro Police Plaza complex. It was bitterly cold, but the dawn sun wasn't too far away. Little good it would do with such snowfall, but it might up the temperature by a degree or two.

"You messaged." The voice seemingly came from nowhere.

"Geez," Sloan started. He saw who it was and his spirits dropped just a bit. "He was too busy to come, huh?"

"The Wraith is..." Lady Wraith began, "...busy with other matters at present."

Sloan eyed her carefully. He wasn't buying it. "For five weeks? C'mon, I know he hasn't been around lately. And he hasn't contacted me in ages, either. What's going on?"

Lady Wraith stood there, still and silent, before finally breaking her silence. "He is missing. I've been searching for him without much success. I may have a lead, though, which I have yet to pursue."

Sloan scratched his head. He didn't know what to say. After a moment, he said, "Geez. Well, if you need help, I'm here."

"This wasn't what you called about," Lady Wraith said.

"No," Sloan said slowly, getting back to the case at hand. "We have a case here...child exploitation. Another Gosch situation. Could be big. The implications are...massive. All the way up the chain. We could use your help."

"Understood. Despite my...other investigation, you can depend on me."

"Really?" Opperman said, appearing from the shadows.

"Hey!" Sloan shouted. "Spying on me isn't part of our deal."

Opperman held up his hands in seeming regret. "I returned to the station with some of my stuff. Nobody knew where you were, and this was the last place I could think of. And here you are with..."

"A friend," Sloan said, still somewhat annoyed. "And a trusted ally. We're gonna need all of those we can get. And she can do things, go places, that we can't."

Opperman didn't look convinced. He was about to speak up, but Sloan cut him off.

"Look, I can vouch for her. She's in and that's final." He turned to Lady Wraith. "Detective Sean Opperman. One of our team."

She nodded. Opperman did not reply and began pacing back and forth. Sloan and Lady Wraith watched on. Finally, "Nearly half a million kids are reported missing each year. Do you realize this?" He continued pacing. "Due to the efforts of the Center for Missing and Exploited Children and the Department of Justice, around ninety-seven percent of those missing children are found and returned to their homes safely."

"Your point, Opperman?" Sloan demanded.

"That leaves fifteen thousand not accounted for. Some you could maybe say slipped detection, but all? No. Some weren't meant to be found. That would ruin everything for those who are a part of this...system. Those who partake of it."

The implications were all too clear, and horrific.

"If we can find Osama bin Laden in a cave," Opperman went on, "Saddam Hussein in a ditch, surely we can find these children–all these children–leaving none of them behind for these...monsters to prey upon."

Lady Wraith took a step toward Opperman. "We will do whatever we can. Nothing less."

She turned and leaped off the roof, disappearing within the snowy squall.

Sloan smiled and turned to Opperman, who hadn't moved, except his mouth, which hung practically down to the ground. "That's nothing," he said with a slight chuckle. "Most of the time they vanish without you even knowing it. C'mon. Let's get inside before we freeze to death."

# ~ Chapter 4 ~

It was morning, but Leena was not in her bed, where she probably should be, resting after a full night's patrol. No, she was in the Lair. Her work was never done. She leaned in and stared at the computer screen. The name and address Fatback had provided her appeared legit. Whether it would lead her to Paul was another matter. But it was the only lead she had.

"You need some rest," a familiar Irish voice said behind her. "You took a leave of absence from the library, you don't need to still be up."

She ignored him, stared absently at the screen in front of her.

Max sighed. "So, did you get anything from Fatback?"

"A possible witness, a Charles Black. Was at some trap house while Paul was there, or at least Fatty thinks so." She tapped at the computer screen, brought some new information up, and suddenly gasped.

Max moved over to her. "What, what is it?"

"The trap house," she said, pointing at the screen. "The location where Fatback thinks Paul was spotted...it's the location of the case Sloan told me about earlier." She went on to fully explain to Max what she knew.

"Are you saying a child sex ring is responsible for Paul's disappearance? I don't see it," Max said.

"They're also involved in drug importation, distribution, weapons imports, perhaps money laundering, and no doubt more. There's wealth behind this, clearly. And people of influence as well."

"That sounds like Latham's sort of thing," Max said, "but he never exploited children, at least not directly, and his empire seems to have run out of steam now that he's dead."

"The point is, big money buys power. Real power. And Paul may have stumbled into that and...and..." She paused. The thought Paul might actually be dead finally hit home. Up until then she had always assumed he'd been captured, held somewhere for some sort of purpose, but now...now it all started to feel so damn hopeless.

"We can't start thinking the Chief is dead," Max said, as though he was somehow able to read Leena's mind. "There's no proof of that. None."

"There's no proof of anything, period," Leena said, still feeling dispirited.

"There's this...Charles Black," Max said. "We start there and see where it takes us."

\* \* \* \* \* \* \*

In a garish pink-and-blue-neon-lit apartment, Robert Anderson lay naked on a bed decorated to match the rest of the surrounding abode. Even though it was roughly the middle of the day, the lamp on the adjacent nightstand was on, rotating several images of magical cartoon creatures all over the wall. There was also the closed drapes.

A naked Asian woman strode in from another room. She was young, but not too young. She plonked herself next to Anderson on the bed, ran her long, painted black fingernails through her equally long, black hair. A dragon tattoo was emblazoned on her right thigh.

"You were pretty intense today," she said.

He grunted.

"Bad day?" she said.

He grunted again.

"I've been your regular for a long time," she said. "You know you can trust me. You can tell me anything."

"Sooki," he broke in. "It's nothing I can talk about. Official business."

"But you know...I hear things. See things. Maybe I can help."

Anderson turned to face her. He'd been seeing her for almost a year. Maybe she was right. Maybe he could take her into his confidence. Maybe...

"How about you?" Anderson tried changing the subject. "Any more problems with your pimp?"

"You can't spell pimple without pimp."

He smirked. She could always make him smile with her nonsense.

"I still think I might be able to help you."

Anderson sat up, frustrated. "All right, all right. We stumbled into a child exploitation ring. The trap house was empty, the perps and victims had flown the coop."

Sooki joined Anderson, sitting upright next to him. "Bent Street?"

He faced her, shocked. "You know of this place?"

"Heard of it, but nothing more. In my line of work, you hear things. Tricks talk, you know?"

Anderson grabbed her by the shoulders, gripped her a little harder than he had intended. "What did you hear? Tell me!"

Sooki struggled to break free. "Hey, you're hurting me, let go!" Her eyes welled up, and Anderson regretted his forcefulness. "I don't know nothing about what goes on there, not really. Obviously, I heard whispers about the kids that went through there, but...I tried blocking all that crap out, you know? But last week, I heard–"

"Yes?" Anderson said impatiently.

Sooki stood and began pacing by the bed. "Look, all I heard was...they had some important person locked up in there."

"A kid?"

"No, no kid," Sooki went on. "An adult. No names, but when the trick let even that info slip...high on drugs as he was, he shut right up after that."

Anderson stood as well, reached down for his pants on the thick, woolen carpet, and pulled them on. It was information, all right, but it didn't really lead in the direction he had wanted. But it was *something*, and he was grateful. He rounded the bed and took Sooki in his arms. "Darling, thank you." He kissed her gently. "Maybe one day...one day I'll be able to–"

She shoved him away. "Yeah, yeah, where have I heard that before? Oh yeah, from a zillion guys."

Anderson frowned. He knew she was right, but her words hurt all the same. With his job, his schedule, his way of life, he found it hard to meet women, and didn't really know what to do with them anyway, apart from the obvious. He'd been with hookers most of his adult life but, somehow, Sooki was different. Or at least he had thought so. Sooki meant something to him. And he thought vice versa. Was he mistaken?

"Hey," Sooki said softly, perhaps realizing her error, "I didn't mean anything by that. I'm still young, but I been around, you know? I...I didn't think I was...good enough for you."

Anderson felt like a heel. He took her in his arms. He vowed that when this case was over, he would take her away from all this. But then his ambitions came back to him. Chief of Police, then...Commissioner? With an ex-hooker by his side? Could he? Would he? He didn't know he had the strength for that. The guts.

Or maybe he just wasn't good enough for her.

* * * * * * *

Charles Black had proven elusive. Not at the address Fatback had supplied, Lady Wraith had bashed a few heads, twisted a few arms, and discovered Black would be at the new Metro Heights Niteclub that night. For what reason? Nobody knew or was willing to say.

So, Leena was there, in the club, undercover, wearing jeans and a hoodie, a backpack containing her Lady Wraith uniform hidden in a storeroom out the back. She was seated at the bar, ostensibly drinking but actually observing. Waiting. The red lights occasionally streamed across her torso as she watched the crowd gyrating; twerking, grinding, and doing just about anything else to what passed for music in the middle of the dance floor. She grew impatient as more of the same occurred and the minutes dragged into hours. At last, Black appeared, resplendently dressed as though he stepped straight out of the 1980s Miami Vice television series. He made his way confidently, smarmy smile in place, through the whirling dervish of people and past them through an open door, which closed quickly behind him.

*Does he work here? For some reason, I never considered that possibility.*

She mulled over her options. Druggie he may be, but judging by his state of dress, Black was well paid, not just some doorman or security guard. A manager or supervisor at the club here? Possibly.

She shoved her glass aside and stood. She gauged the room he had entered to be on the club's west side. This part of the club was on the second floor. She knew what her next move would be and strode toward the storeroom at the back of the club.

\* \* \* \* \* \* \*

Black sat at a large desk within his office and opened the top right drawer, bringing out a small tray with a line of white powder placed there, and laid it gently on his desk. He smiled as he prepared for his nightly hit.

\* \* \* \* \* \* \*

Suddenly, the window exploded in a hail of glass and Lady Wraith appeared, thudding onto Black's desk. He screamed and flung himself to his left, off his leather chair and onto the floor. Before he could look up, before he had a chance to make sense of it all, his office was thrust into darkness, and Lady Wraith discreetly locked his office door.

"Wha...who is this? Whatya want?" he cried in panic.

From the darkness, two Eyes burst to electrical life, casting an eerie, sickening yellow sheen to the room. He knew who this was, Lady Wraith saw...and he was afraid.

"Where is The Wraith?" Lady Wraith boomed, her voice a mix of Lauren Bacall and something electronic.

She was back up on his desk and yanked Black up off the floor, gripping him by his expensive suit collar.

"The...The Wraith?" he said, blatantly fearful for his life. "I don't know anything about The Wraith. I thought you were..."

"The trap house on Bent Street. You were seen there. The Wraith was seen there. You know what's going on. Talk!" Her face was right before his.

Black gulped. The mere mention of that place clearly struck a nerve Lady Wraith couldn't help but notice.

"B...Bent Street? I ain't never been there."

She yanked him harder into her face, practically spat as she spoke. "You lie!"

"Okay, okay," he said. "I been there. I get my stash there, direct." He indicated to the powdery mess on the floor beside him. "But I never seen The Wraith there. A bunch of kids were there, sure, but they were hidden away, and some other guy, my dealer there mentioned him, but he never gave a name and I never saw him."

Furious, Lady Wraith threw Black to the floor. The Eyes on her chest continued to burn bright. "You know more. Tell me!"

Black, on his rear, inched his way backwards as far as he could go before smacking into the wall. "I don't know anything more, I swear!"

"Tell me about the trap house," Lady Wraith said. "Who's back of it? Who's ultimately responsible for what goes on there?"

Black started to sweat. Profusely. He knew more than he was letting on. "I...I can't tell you. I'm a dead man if I say anything. I got loved ones, a family."

"You won't live beyond this room if you don't tell me something I want to hear!"

"Then I'm a dead man anyway, and I don't have to say a damn thing."

Enraged, she punched him in the gut, bending him over, Black trying to hack and heave the breath back into himself. As his attention was diverted, Lady Wraith noticed what appeared to be some sort of door to the side of the room; not the office door she had locked.

Heavy knocks started raining down on the office door. "Mr. Black, sir, are you okay?"

Lady Wraith yanked Black upright. "That door," she indicated to her side. "Where does it lead?"

Still coughing, while the knocks at the front door became loud bashing, Black managed, "It's...an...elevator."

She grabbed him and dragged him over to the elevator door. A keypad to its left indicated it was password protected.

"What's the passcode?" Lady Wraith demanded.

Black remained silent and still.

"Now!" She pulled his arm behind his back and ripped upwards. An audible snap indicated the breaking of bone.

Black screamed and quickly acquiesced. With his other hand, he carefully punched in the passcode. As the elevator door opened, the office door crashed open and three armed thugs stormed in.

Lady Wraith flung Black inside and jumped to follow. The door closed behind them as gunfire smacked into the door.

"Where does this lead?" Lady Wraith said, but Black refused to answer. There were only two buttons on the console: O for Office and B for...Basement? B it was. Down they went.

# ~ Chapter 5 ~

Sloan slammed the phone back into its cradle. He was livid. He truly didn't know what to think at this latest development, even though he had half expected it.

"Whoa, whoa," Anderson said as he and Opperman entered the main workroom of Metro Police Plaza.

"I know that look," Opperman said.

Sloan looked up at him and didn't doubt him for one second. Not after what he'd been told of the Gosch case.

"I just spoke with Harrison on the phone," Sloan said. "The Feds are coming and they have full jurisdiction over the entire case. We're completely out in the cold."

Opperman nodded. "They'll be here shortly, initially friendly and conciliatory, then they'll lock us out. Harshly."

Sloan and Anderson both viewed Opperman with some incredulity.

Opperman smirked. "It's always the same. They use the same playbook over and over again. The feds will storm in, take over the case, pronounce some great overtures about not letting anyone get away with this, then proceed to make a few, perfunctory arrests, and wala...case closed. And everyone of note gets away with it. Always the same."

Sloan heard out Opperman's spiel then beckoned his two colleagues to sit. "Right. I had hoped against hope we wouldn't have to do this, or at least had more time officially on this case, but, as discussed, we go underground. Officially, we smile, do as we're told, but we handle the case ourselves, just the three of us. And those we trust."

Both Anderson and Opperman nodded their agreement.

"Until the FBI get here, which is likely tomorrow morning, we continue as normal." He took a deep breath. "What do we have so far? Anything about this trap house? Any leads on this P.S.?"

"As we thought," Opperman said, "the apartment was owned by some dummy corporations, linked to more dummy corporations and false names and so on. We *could* eventually trace it back to someone meaningful, perhaps, but it would take time, and those records will likely be expunged before then...if they haven't already."

"Dammit!" Sloan said. "What about the neighbor that initially called it in?"

"She's an elderly lady," Anderson said, "and didn't seem to know anything more than her initial report. She did appear very nervous when I interviewed her earlier, but then, some people do get nervy around cops." He paused before continuing. "I do have one good source who did provide me some interesting information."

"Go on," Sloan said, eager to hear more.

"Apparently an adult was being held prisoner there, not just children. Someone big was the way they were described. What that means or who they're talking about...I just don't know."

"Could this P.S. be the adult in question?" Opperman surmised aloud.

Sloan eye's bulged wide. What a fool he'd been. P.S. *Of course*. It all made sense.

He jumped to his feet and made for the exit.

"Hey!" Anderson cried after him. "What gives?"

"I'll be back," Sloan cried back. "I just thoughta something. Hang tight."

\* \* \* \* \* \* \*

The elevator door opened with a whooshing of gears. Overhead lights streamed on, one after the other in a lengthy sequence, revealing a massive warehouse-like structure. As Black whimpered beside her in pain, Lady Wraith took in the sight before her: row after row of large wooden crates. Some were square in shape, many more rectangular. Some were stacked at least ten-high in places.

"What do you have stored here?" Lady Wraith said.

He remained silent, save for his whimpering. Lady Wraith shook him from his stupor.

"What is all this?"

"W...weapons mostly, imports from the Middle East, some records," Black said.

"Records? Of what?"

He clammed shut at that.

"Of what?" she said again, slamming Black into the closed elevator door, broken arm first.

He winced hard from what was no doubt a shockwave of pain. "Client lists mostly. Who paid for the weapons, where they're to go, that sort of thing. And..." Black gulped, appearing not willing to go any further.

Lady Wraith knew how to handle that. She clutched at his dead arm and pulled further. Black screamed in utter agony. "What are you not telling me?"

"S...some client lists of...of...Bent Street. Records of the victims."

"The children?" Lady Wraith ripped at his injured arm some more.

"Y...yes!"

*Now we're getting somewhere*, Lady Wraith thought.

"Which crates hold the records?"

"I don't know, they're just stored here, I have nothing to do with them myself."

"Yet you have a personal elevator that takes you right down here," Lady Wraith said, scoffing. Nevertheless, she did believe him. "There must be another way down here?" She dropped the hapless Black to the floor.

"And they'll be here any minute," he shrieked. "You're dead, woman. Dead!"

He was no doubt right. Paid thugs would be storming in there from somewhere, guns ablaze, shooting at anything that moved. Black would undoubtedly be in their line of fire as well. She hadn't much time to act.

She retrieved from her belt a small hand-held digital scanner. If there were any digital files within these crates, this device–as Max had described to her–would detect them and scan and retrieve those files, storing them on a SD card stored within the scanner. Quickly, she held the device aloft, passed it over crate after crate. She moved as quickly as she could but, thus far, no result.

A few more minutes passed. Sweat began to flow beneath her cowl. Then, a hit. Her scanner beeped and a progress chart appeared on the tiny viewscreen. Thirty percent, forty, fifty. A few seconds more and the data was retrieved. She repeated the process over more crates. And a few more...before all hell broke loose.

Armed guards appeared at the far end of the vast underground warehouse. Lady Wraith ducked behind a row of crates, kept her breath in check. Her escape was blocked in that direction. There was no more time to gather evidence. Her mind turned to an escape plan.

"She's over here!" Black yelled, still laying on the floor.

Gunfire exploded in his direction. She was not wrong. They were going to shoot at anything and everything. Nothing and nobody were safe.

The elevator. It was Lady Wraith's only avenue to get out. Black's bullet-riddled body lay next to its door, blood flowing toward and under it. Lady Wraith knew the passcode; she had watched Black intently as he keyed it in earlier. Her uniform would offer some protection from the barrage to come, but uzis? In such high numbers? She could only pray that Max had excelled beyond the norm when he had designed and created hers.

She produced a pellet from her belt and lobbed it up and over her vantage point toward the gathering horde. Smoke erupted from the floor beneath their feet, causing instant chaos and confusion. In response, they let loose with their weapons, firing in all directions.

Lady Wraith leapt from her position, keyed in the correct code, and waited for the door to open. She felt two bullets slam into her back, causing her great pain, but she could tell her cloak had held firm. The door opened and she slipped inside, ensuring the door closed quickly behind her.

She was safe...for a time. She hoped that nobody had remained in Black's office to stand guard, but perhaps that was too much to hope for.

The elevator door opened, and bullets plunged in. Lady Wraith remained inside, hugging the side wall. With a flurry and a swish of her cloak, she was out, had disarmed the sole gunman, and sent him to sleep.

*Thank goodness there was only one.*

Her communicator buzzed. It was the special line. Sloan. She sighed, but it was good timing all the same. They had much to talk about. Without another thought, she went over to the open window, peered out and sent a grapnel line up toward the roof. In seconds, she was shooting up and onwards to freedom.

\* \* \* \* \* \* \*

Sloan paced energetically from side-to-side on the snowy rooftop. He was severely agitated. Back and forth he marched, waiting, brooding.

"What is it now?" Lady Wraith said.

Sloan jumped. He was used to this routine The Wraith–and now Lady Wraith–consistently pulled, but yet was always taken by surprise. "You're getting good at that. You have a good teacher."

"Do you have any new information?"

"As a matter of fact," Sloan said, excited, "I do. The trap house on Bent Street. We found some initials carved into a wooden post down in the basement. Too tall to have been made by a child. P.S."

Lady Wraith took a backward step, clearly stunned by the news.

"This correlates with The Wraith's disappearance. Our first lead on that front," Sloan continued. "He must have stumbled onto the situation there."

Silence. Lady Wraith merely stood there, her mouth agape.

Sloan looked around, checked they were alone. It appeared they were. Even so, he lowered his voice. "I know Paul is The Wraith. I also know he was once Michael Reeve...Leena."

More silence.

"How?" she finally said. "When?"

"I've known for a while, but I can't really tell you how. I had some sort of a...vision, I guess you'd call it. Around the time the citywide depression started affecting people's mood. I don't know how or why...all I *do* know is that from that moment on, I've felt more myself. Better even."

This was developing into more of a confessional from Sloan than from Lady Wraith. It was something he needed to get off his chest for quite some time, he realized.

"So, The Wraith...Paul...*was* being held prisoner in this trap house," Lady Wraith said, getting back onto topic. "I can only hope they haven't yet unmasked him, but perhaps that's a forlorn hope." She paused, clearly taking a moment to think, then continued. "I've been able to ascertain his last verified location was near the abandoned Christopher Docks."

Sloan rubbed his chin. "We know weapons come through there. We've just lacked the manpower to–"

"Not just weapons, Sloan, but drugs, and, I suspect, human trafficking."

It was Sloan's turn to be shocked. "You mean...children, imported for trap houses like Bent Street?"

Lady Wraith nodded.

"I...I just assumed it would be more local kids, but...it makes sense. Demand is probably outstripping local supply."

"It's no doubt easier to make kids disappear from Mexico or India or..." She couldn't finish her sentence.

Sloan knew what she felt. He felt it, too. The revulsion, the sense of helpfulness, the urge to rescue the children and seek justice.

"I have some evidence here," she said, holding a handheld device aloft for Sloan to see. "I need to go through it first before I share. But you might want to send a raiding party to the Metro Heights Niteclub. And you'll want to do it quickly."

"That seedy fleabag?" Sloan said. "Why there?"

"It's connected to the trap house," Lady Wraith said. "The club is acting as a storage facility for weapons imported through the Christopher Docks. And there are records there pertaining to the child exploitation ring."

Sloan gasped. He knew what that meant for the case.

"Very important records."

* * * * * * *

Back at the Lair, Leena sat at the computer terminal, transferring the data from her scanner to the main computer. It took a few seconds, and when it was done she murmured her approval. As the records began to appear on her screen, the Sanderson butler, Jonathan Simpson, appeared with a breakfast tray and placed it on the desk beside her.

"I thought you might like a little something," Simpson said. He was tall, distinguished looking but also a somewhat taciturn individual. A veteran of the 1990 Gulf War, he ran the household with a strict, but friendly, hand.

Names and photos scrolled up the screen in steady procession. Beautiful little faces appeared and disappeared, replaced by more of the same. Tears streamed down Leena's face. Man's inhumanity to man knew no bounds. A few minutes more and the names and faces of children were replaced with those of adults. The client list. Suddenly, the screen went black. Leena grunted in frustration. Obviously the list was incomplete, but she had run out of time in obtaining them. And no word of Paul, not that she had truly expected any. But then hope had a funny way of working on one's mind.

"I have to back all this up," she said, and proceeded to do so as she finally acknowledged Simpson standing beside her. "Oh, Simpson."

"Miss," he replied. "A little breakfast for you."

She blankly looked down at the tray. A pot of coffee, which admittedly smelled delicious, and some croissants and jelly. Under normal circumstances, she would have devoured them, but today? Today was different. She didn't feel like doing much of anything except finding Paul and seeking justice for all those helpless, innocent children.

"I need to get these over to Sloan," Leena said, indicating toward the computer screen. "We have enough names here to blow this case wide open. Now it's his turn."

The red line on her terminal began buzzing. It was Sloan again. His timing was always impeccable. She reached for the headphones by the right side of the screen and placed them over her head.

"Sloan, I have something–" Leena started.

"Turn on your TV," Sloan cried out, a cacophony of screaming and sirens audible in the background. "They beat us there."

Leena did so without another thought, flicking screens on her terminal. MNN came into view, and the sight horrified her. The Metro Heights Niteclub was ablaze. Firefighters were already on the scene, attacking the site valiantly, but it was already too late. As Leena watched, the club's roof caved in, sparks firing upwards and outwards, causing even the onsite journalists to flee back for safety. Simpson watched closely beside her, the carnage even affecting his stoicism.

"Whatever was there," Sloan yelled above the din, "is of little or no use to us. But we'll retrieve whatever—"

As he spoke, a massive explosion rung out, flame and debris spewing—the TV screen suddenly went black.

"Sloan? Sloan!" Leena cried.

The line was dead.

\* \* \* \* \* \* \*

The heat was unbearable. A searing heat, almost like one was being turned over a flame like a chicken on a rotisserie. Turn it off, turn it—

"Yahh!" Sloan came to with a start, sat bolt upright. Where was he, what had happened?

He tried clearing his eyes, scanned the nearby area. Though his vision was blurred, he could make out he was surrounded by the wounded—police and other emergency personnel for the most part—though Heaven only knew how many people were caught in the inferno inside. Blood filled his field of view, staining the snow around him a nightmarish crimson. He tried to stand, then fell back down with a thud, the pain in his right leg becoming apparent, coursing through him like a jackhammer. He checked his thigh. There was a chunk of something embedded in it. A lot of the blood he saw was his own. He knew better than to touch or try to remove whatever it was.

His head cleared a bit. He tried to stand again, pushing through the agony, forcing himself to his feet. The cries of pain and anguish filled his ears. The scene was akin to that of a warzone. The sound of distant sirens rose and soon grew louder as more emergency personnel were dispatched to the disaster zone.

Sloan gritted his teeth, inched his way through the snow and debris. The dead and wounded were all around him. The explosion had not only taken out the club, but almost the entire block. Ambulances and more firefighters had now arrived. Two paramedics tried to force Sloan onto a gurney, but he was having none of it.

"I'm fine, I'm fine," he muttered. "See to the wounded. Over there." He waved them away.

"What the hell happened here?" Anderson said, exiting his car, Opperman in tow.

"You guys finally made it," Sloan muttered. "You take the scenic route? This was a raid pertaining to the case."

Anderson appeared chagrined. "We were questioning some potential witnesses, Opperman insisted we..."

"Never mind, never mind," Sloan said, waving their excuses away. "Whatever evidence may have been inside is no longer available to us. We're back to square one."

His anger fueled his adrenalin, causing his thigh to bleed further. He teetered to one side, Anderson grabbing him by the arm, preventing his fall.

"Whoa, you need to get to a hospital," Opperman said as he took Sloan's other arm. "Paramedic!"

Sloan tried to argue, tried to fight, but there was no longer any fight left in him. He felt faint.

Blackness loomed.

# ~ Chapter 6 ~

**W**hen Sloan finally awoke, he found himself lying in a hospital bed in a darkened room. There was no one about. The shrapnel had been removed, and he was all bandaged up. He felt terrific, better than terrific. Even with his brain in a muddle, he knew he was on one heck of a painkiller trip.

He tried to shake the cobwebs loose.

"I'm glad you made it," a female voice said from the corner of the room. A shape emerged from the shadows.

Lady Wraith.

"You're getting *really* good at this," Sloan said.

"I've had practice."

"Look," Sloan said, his mind awhirl, "you don't have to worry. Your secret–Paul's secret–is safe with me."

"I know," Lady Wraith said softly. "I know. I never thought otherwise." She smiled ever-so-slightly, which Sloan thought looked weird as hell, then she removed something from her belt. "Take this. It's incomplete, but there's enough names on here to make a lot of arrests. And hopefully save a lot of lives." She placed a USB flash drive into his left hand and gently closed his fingers over it. "Don't lose it."

He looked down at the drive in his hand and smiled. Some good news at last. When he looked back up to thank her, she was gone.

* * * * * * *

The light flickered incessantly, causing the magical creatures to blink in and out of focus. Anderson rubbed his eyes. Damn thing was giving him a headache. He reached over to the lamp, and hurled it into the wall, smashing it into a million pieces.

"Hey, that was a gift from my mom," Sooki wailed, leaping from the bed alongside her lover.

Anderson sat up. "I'm sorry. It's just this case. We're getting nowhere, Sloan was injured, and now the feds are stepping in."

Sooki said nothing. She crouched down, trying to pick up the pieces of her lamp.

"Something doesn't feel right," Anderson said after a moment. "I don't know what it is, but..."

"There's too many pieces," Sooki sobbed, holding a few of the larger portions aloft. "I can't even glue it all back together."

"Yeah," Anderson continued, "there's something not right. But I can't yet put my finger on it."

"You want a finger?" Sooki said angrily. "Here's one." She flipped him off.

He stood and took her in his arms, silencing her protests.

\* \* \* \* \* \* \*

He's running, desperately trying to flee, to make his escape, but his legs aren't working properly. He cannot get up to full speed. It was as if he was running through a morass of mud. Which way to turn? This way? No, the other. He swiveled and headed into the dark, narrow passageway. But no, it was a dead end. He turned. Another dead end faced him. He was trapped, there was no way out. He tried to scream but nothing came out. He was mute, helpless. Then, shadowy, ghostly figures emerged from the nothingness, loomed before and around him, their garish visages slowly coming into view. It was the Cobra, Aztekoth, Dr. Satanish, Crossfire. Then, Robert Latham appeared, and laughed, mockingly, horribly, and...

Leena awoke with a jolt, sweat pouring from her brow. She tried to wipe it away with her hands but all she managed to do was smear it up and through her hair. The nightmare was fast becoming a regular occurrence, and it was always the same. Paul fleeing, helpless, unable to escape, surrounded by his enemies with no one there to help him. That was how she felt right now–helpless. She looked to her Rolex Oyster Perpetual wristwatch. It was 11AM. Only a few hours' sleep, but with such disturbed sleep, she felt she was better off being awake. She looked to the bedside dresser on Paul's side of the bed. His new Héron Marinor dive watch, which Max had only recently supplied him with during their time in Satan's Forest, lay there. She picked it up, gazed at it, tears in her eyes, and wondered why he hadn't been wearing it. Another mystery to add to the pile.

She dressed quickly and made her way downstairs. She bumped into Simpson at the bottom.

"Good morning, Miss Leena," he said.

"Morning," she replied, striding past him. "No breakfast, Simpson. Just some coffee. I'll be in the Lair."

Leena marched through the house, into Paul's study, reached into the right-hand top drawer of his desk and retrieved a small remote control device. Pressing the button, a section of the bookcase pushed forward, a whooshing of gears, and then slid to one side, revealing a dark, cavernous entryway. She stepped inside, the bookcase sliding back into place behind her.

Powerful overhead spotlights snapped on, revealing the Lair in all its futuristic glory. She was atop a metal gangway that circled the perimeter of the structure, with a metal staircase before her, which she swiftly descended. In a moment, she was at the massive computer terminal and began punching at the keyboard. The screen lit up with names and photos. It was the client list.

*There must be something here*, Leena thought. *Something that will link back to Paul. There has to be.*

She thoroughly scanned each entry. There were many names she recognized, some which shocked even her, others were unknown, but nothing seemed to have any sort of connection with Paul, nothing seemed to register with her. She continued, read every word, let nothing slip through.

Then, all at once, it hit her. She gasped. There was Charlie Grieco's name, Latham's former lieutenant, and recently murdered by Crossfire. She read on. So, Grieco was secretly a pedophile, had a penchant for young boys. The younger the better. Leena wretched up a mouthful of bile.

*Was Latham aware of this? Is that why he had Grieco jailed?*

There was no way of knowing, and it wouldn't make any difference to the case at hand if she did. But wait...even with Latham and Grieco gone, the organization, albeit diminished, remained. Could Latham Industries be responsible for Paul's disappearance? Could they also be somehow involved with the child exploitation ring, even if only peripherally? It would make a strange sort of sense. Who was running things over at Latham Industries now?

*Patrich Azufi,* Leena recalled. *Of course. Despite his recent injuries, he's been trying to right the good ship Latham. Any link between the organization and a pedophile ring—even if it was only via Grieco—has to be hidden at all costs. And, no doubt, much of the drugs and weaponry stored at the club was imported by Latham and-or Azufi. As with his predecessor, much of the organization's wealth was derived from the sale of drugs and weapons.* She stood and paced, ideas swarming through her head. *With Latham Industries in such perilous shape recently, perhaps that's also why Azufi teamed up with these pedophile scum, despite the risks involved.*

Leena let everything percolate in her mind. That had to be it. Azufi, somehow, was responsible for Paul's disappearance and was no doubt keeping him prisoner somewhere. Firstly, at the trap house, perhaps only as a starting point, and then...somewhere more secure? It was all conjecture, of course, but at this stage it was all she had to go on, and she needed to pursue it.

Patrich Azufi would be receiving a visit–from Lady Wraith.

\* \* \* \* \* \* \*

A murky sun beat down on the still-newish Metro Police Plaza complex, highlighting its fresh paintwork and steel balustrades. A taxicab screeched to a halt in front and Sloan limped out, quickly paying the driver. He looked up at the complex. It was a nice enough building, certainly in better condition than the original, but it somehow lacked a certain...feeling, to his mind. As dilapidated as the original had been, it still somehow felt like...home? Or something close enough to it. This new one was almost too...antiseptic. But that was modern architecture for you.

A few moments later and he was inside and upstairs, nearing his desk.

"You look like crap," Anderson said seated at Sloan's desk, looking through some paperwork. Opperman sat before him at Perez's desk. "Shouldn't you still be in hospital?"

"You got your own desk," Sloan said. "It's just a scratch." He leaned over and whispered, "The three of us will talk later."

"Later is right," Opperman said. "The commissioner wants to see you."

"How did he know I'd be here today?" Sloan said, plopping down into his chair now that Anderson had vacated it.

"He must know how stubborn you are," Opperman said, winking to Anderson.

"Okay, okay," Sloan said. He struggled getting back up. His thigh stung. He refused further painkillers when he checked himself out of the hospital. All that stuff did was dull the brain, or so he told himself.

He made his way slowly over to Harrison's office, which was located at the far end of the main workroom and around the corner. He knocked and entered.

"You asked to...see me?"

Commissioner George Harrison was inside seated at his desk, his trademark hairpiece not in position. This was serious, then. Standing before Harrison was a tall, younger man with short-cropped brown hair and outfitted in a close-fitting dark grey suit. He turned to face Sloan.

"I knew you wouldn't stay away long, Sloan, you stubborn old fool," Harrison said. He stood to greet his detective. "Even if that leg had been blown off, you'd be back here in no time getting on with the job."

"Such dedication to the job is commendable," the younger man said with a smile.

"This is Agent Gibbs," Harrison introduced. "From the FBI."

Gibbs reached out a hand and took Sloan's with a firm, assured shake, continuing to smile, which irked Sloan to no end. "Frank Gibbs," Gibbs said. "My team is here, and Commissioner Harrison has fully briefed us on the case thus far."

Sloan looked Gibbs up and down. He was dressed like a typical fed. Maybe not straight out of Quantico, but he made a passing resemblance of it.

"I have everything you and your team has assembled, and we'll be taking it from here. We won't let these scum get away with this," Gibbs said. It all sounded just like Opperman had described.

"Of course," Sloan said in mock deference. "If there's anything you need, my team of detectives are here to help in any way."

"Thank you, that's most kind, but not needed. My team is better equipped to deal with such matters, and we have much more experience with it. If you remember the Gosch case...that was one of our most successful apprehensions. We left no stone unturned and made history. Everyone responsible was locked away for decades."

Sloan knew that was only partially true. *Very* partially true, but he nodded in agreement, feigning a sense of being impressed.

"You and your men can go about your daily work. We'll take it from here," Gibbs said again as if a way of telling Sloan he could leave.

Sloan looked to Harrison who nodded. Sloan faked a smile and retreated from the office.

\* \* \* \* \* \* \*

It was late afternoon and the sun was slowly retreating behind the city's skyscrapers, the buildings acting as intermittent tentacles blocking out the light. Slivers of sunshine burst forth here and there, illuminating narrow sections of the street like incandescent tendrils.

Sloan guided his ramshackle vehicle into the alley, stopped it suddenly and exited, pulling on his trademark Metro City Lions baseball cap. He leaned up against the car and waited. Moments later, another, newer and in better condition, car appeared and parked alongside him.

"It was as you said," Sloan started once Anderson and Opperman appeared from their car. "The feds have taken over, and we've been shut down."

"Standard FBI operating procedure," Opperman said.

"So, what do we do now?" Anderson piped up.

"Just as we planned," Sloan said. "We knew this was coming and now we have...this." He held up the USB flash drive for the others to see.

"What's this?" Anderson asked.

"Evidence. Records of both victims and those who prey upon them"

"No way," Anderson said.

"Wait, wait, how did you get that?" Opperman said, dumbfounded. "The night club was destroyed before any of us could get in there."

Anderson eyed Opperman intently.

"I have my sources, don't you remember? A special member of our team."

"Wait, what?" Anderson said, confused.

"That woman...Lady Wraith?" Opperman said.

Sloan nodded.

"I still don't know if I'm ready to trust her. She's a vigilante," Opperman said.

"I'd trust her with my life. End of conversation," Sloan said firmly.

"I assume, then, that we *don't* hand these records over to the FBI," Anderson said.

"Hell no," Opperman said. "We'd just be playing into their hands. They'd destroy the evidence and sacrifice a few of the small fry to try and make everything appear on the up-and-up. Case solved."

"And closed," Sloan said. "Opperman's right. We're on our own with this."

"But what can we do?" Anderson said. "We lack the manpower to make...how many arrests? To follow...how many leads?"

"We have enough," Sloan said. "You're underestimating our colleagues. Harrison–and The Wraith–cut a swath through the dirty cops in our outfit, remember?"

"Yes, but the feds..." Anderson started.

"Won't be able to stop us once we make the arrests, present the evidence, and maybe get the media on our side," Sloan said. "I know Gayle Rodgers would kill for an exclusive like this."

Anderson considered it for a moment then nodded in agreement. Sloan handed Opperman the flash drive.

"Here, you take this. You and Anderson start going through the names. Then, we go after these sons of bitches."

# ~ Chapter 7 ~

Lady Wraith crouched atop the Latham Industries building. It was late, but Patrich Azufi was still at work, located in his office several floors below. With the bug she had secreted there earlier, she heard him shuffling papers, talking on the phone, making sexual advances toward his secretary. A typical day at the office.

Before too long, he finally said he was on his way home. Lady Wraith readied herself. "Max, do you read me?"

"Loud and clear," came the reply.

"Our bird is about to fly. I'll meet you in the alley."

She lowered herself by grapnel line down into the alley that ran along the south side of the Latham building. Max had the Daimler there, ready and waiting.

"The beacon is in place," he said as she took her seat in the back. "We'll be able to follow them no matter where they go."

"Good."

A radar on the car's dash indicated in green the location of Azufi's car. He wasn't too far ahead of them. Max piloted the car out into the late-night traffic and made to follow at a discreet distance. As long as the beacon was in operation, they need not keep Azufi in visual range.

Traffic was surprisingly tight, given the lateness of the hour, but that was Metro City for you. The city never slept. Indeed, it was only late at night the city came truly to life, for better or worse.

Mostly worse.

"Uh oh, here's an interesting development," Max said, watching the radar screen intently.

"He's not heading home?"

"He most certainly is not," Max said. "He's currently living in Broadside with that...nurse friend of his."

"And he's heading in the opposite direction," Lady Wraith continued. "Toward...the docks?"

"The waterfront at any rate," Max said. "What could he be doing there, I wonder?"

"Let's find out."

* * * * * * *

Azufi's limousine parked alongside a rundown warehouse, one of many such buildings in the docklands area. Azufi alighted from the back seat, casually looked around, then lit a cigarette. He took a few draws then ambled over to a door on the side of the warehouse. He entered.

Inside was row after row of crates, though not tidily stacked. It looked like they were stored there in a hurry. Some of the crates appeared damaged: dented and splintered.

"What the f–"

"Mr Azufi, sir." A low-life thug appeared from the shadows. "We didn't know you were coming." Other such thugs joined him in the light.

"Is any of this merchandise damaged? It's worth a fortune. Sales of this shipment alone will get me back on top," Azufi said. "You should have taken better care."

"We were in a hurry," a deep voice boomed from the shadows. As he emerged, Azufi couldn't help but gasp. It was a mountain of a man, tall and as broad as a wardrobe. Muscles upon muscles. He was outfitted in grey tactical armor from head to foot. A red cobra was emblazoned on his upper left chest. A mask akin to that of a hockey goalkeeper hid his identity from all and sundry. "We did not have time to *take care.*"

"B...Blackstorm," Azufi said. "I didn't know you'd be here. W...where's our...special package?"

"Under wraps. I took...better care of him."

Azufi breathed a sigh of relief. "Thank goodness. His unmasking will make me an absolute fortune. Who knows how high the bids will get when we go live online."

Blackstorm took a step closer to Azufi. "I am not concerned with such things."

"Ah...yes...okay..." was all Azufi could get out.

"His worth to me is not monetary," Blackstorm added. "What he has done, to my master...that I cannot brook."

"Okay," Azufi said, "whatever."

"Whatta we do now, Mr. Azufi?" the thug who spoke earlier asked.

"Hold tight," Azufi said. "I have to arrange transportation for all these crates so we can set up a viewing with our potential buyers. No one of any worth or consequence will come *here*. Too risky. As for The Wraith...I'll leave that to you, Blackstorm. Keep him safe. Bids will commence in five days."

Before another word could be said, the above skylight detonated in a series of small charges, sending shards of glass plummeting around and over them. A bold, shadowy figure, followed suit, landing amongst them.

"Lady Wraith," Azufi gasped, fear engulfing him.

* * * * * * *

Lady Wraith landed in the middle of her intended prey. Azufi careened backwards on his haunches, panic etched into his features. Azufi's thugs attempted to fight back, but Lady Wraith made quick work of them. First, she disarmed them both, then let loose with powerful punches, one after the other. She then turned to Azufi, who was now pressed as hard against the warehouse wall as his skinny frame allowed.

"No, no..." he whimpered, "stay back."

"Patrich Azufi," Lady Wraith moaned. "Your time of judgment is at hand." The Eyes on her chest burst to life. Though they were inventions of Max's, and were built into the suit he had crafted and did not act as The Wraith's Judgment Stare; their visual impact alone often had the desired affect amongst the evil.

"I think not," a voice boomed behind her.

She swiveled and came face-to-face with a mountain of a man. She gasped inwardly at the sight of the red cobra on his chest. Could it mean...

"Blackstorm," Azufi cried out. "Take care of this for me." He turned and ran for the exit.

"I had hoped to face The Wraith himself in combat, but he is...otherwise detained," Blackstorm said with a snigger. "I have other things planned for him, but you will suffice in the meantime."

"What have you done with him?" Lady Wraith demanded. "Where is he?"

Blackstorm cackled. "He is here. He is alive. You will have to come through me to get to him. Are you able to defeat me? My death is the only way you can rescue your man." He waved with his hands for her to come to him. He clearly relished a fight.

And Lady Wraith would give him one.

She stepped forward, but cautiously at first. No doubt this...Blackstorm...counted on her taking the offensive, rushing into battle without a thought, and he would then make quick work of her. She had no intention of bending to his wishes. If Paul was here, she would save him. She *had* to.

She pulled a pellet from her belt and lobbed it at Blackstorm's feet, smoke erupting up and around him, fully enveloping him. She entered the fray, jumping forth and letting loose with a barrage of blows. Blackstorm, confused and blinded, could do nothing but receive hit after hit. Lady Wraith connected with a kick to the torso, punches to the body and face and, finally, Blackstorm's legs were swept out from under him.

"Take me to The Wraith!" Lady Wraith said. "Or I will inflict such harm upon you–"

Blackstorm flipped himself back onto his feet from his back–the Chinese get-up–and laughed. "You are not the whimpering simp I had expected." He readied himself.

"Nevertheless, your blows caused me no harm at all. Mine, on the other hand, will break you in two!"

He rushed her, taking Lady Wraith completely off guard. How could a man of such size move so fast? With one hand, he lifted her clear off the ground and smacked her face with his other, sending her pummeling to the floor. She felt at her jaw and wondered if it was broken.

*He's so strong. I don't know if I can take him.*

She staggered to her feet, but he was too quick for her again. Before she could gather her senses, he was upon her, raining blow after blow. Blood spattered from her mouth, dripped from her nose. The onslaught continued until Lady Wraith, pain overwhelming her, thought she was done for, thought, briefly but horribly so, that perhaps death would actually be a blessing.

*No, it can't end like this*, she thought. *Not when Paul needs me, and the city needs him, more than ever before.*

Blackstorm, holding her aloft once more, smashed her entire body into the warehouse wall, cracking the wall in several places and causing the entire edifice to shudder. This was it.

*No, wait! My own Judgment Stare.*

She wrenched her stronger left arm free and began smashing at her assailant's face. Again and again. Finally, she reached down to her belt.

*Right button blinds.*

She pressed a button on her belt. The Eyes of Judgment on her chest flashed a brilliant, fiery yellow, bursting forth into Blackstorm's line of sight.

"Arrghhh!" he screamed, staggering back, his hands up at his eyes. "You blinded me! You'll pay for this."

Lady Wraith was free but had trouble standing. She took a few deep breaths on her knees and then tried again to stand.

She was up. Blackstorm was before her, flailing about, cursing, rubbing at his eyes. With every ounce of her strength, she lashed at her opponent with a kick to the groin. His cursing instantly stopped, replaced by a stilted groaning, and down he went.

Quickly, Lady Wraith staggered about, trying to find a door to some sort of backroom and, finally, she found one. She plummeted through to find...nothing. It was empty.

Desperately, she searched through every inch of the warehouse but found no other room, no other space where The Wraith might be held. She was forced to finally realize Blackstorm her lied to her. A criminal lying...what a concept.

Returning to the backroom, she scanned the area for any clues. Perhaps Paul had been held there earlier. Or maybe he had never been there at all? But she had to make sure, or as sure as she could possibly be.

The room was empty of anything save dust. At least dozens of footprints were evident, most of whom belonged to Blackstorm judging by their size, but there were a few that looked familiar to her. They were faint, as though their owner could barely stand. Indeed, they were preceded by lengthy drag marks, but she nevertheless could make out a weak tread...and she knew it was The Wraith's. He *had* been there.

*And what's that? Over there.*

Slight scratch marks. Only barely visible from a certain angle, and partially obliterated by footsteps, but she could still make it out. *P.S.* again.

*Paul's always letting me know where he's been. But where is he now?* She paused. *These marks appear fresh.*

Filled with rage, she stormed from the backroom back into the warehouse with the intent of making Blackstorm talk. But he was gone. Had he regained his sight already? Or, even without sight, had he managed to find the exit and make his escape? She raced to the door and peered out into the night. There was no sign of him.

"Dammit!" she grunted. A few more deep breaths then she lurched backwards, realizing she was more hurt than she thought. With her adrenalin dropping, the pain was coming to the fore. She sagged to her knees. Unconsciousness was imminent. Quickly, she tapped at her temple, activating her comm-link.

"Max...I need you here."

All went black.

\* \* \* \* \* \* \*

Anderson and Opperman were in their unmarked heading back to Metro Police Plaza. Anderson was at the wheel.

"What a break," Anderson said, upbeat. "With that flash drive we can break this case wide open. Really nail those bastards."

"Let's see what we have first before we go pronouncing this case closed," Opperman said.

Anderson turned briefly to closely watch his colleague. "What gives? I thought you were eager to finally get some justice."

Opperman sighed. "It's not that. I am. It's just that...I've come this close before only to have the rug pulled out from under me. I've learned to take things cautiously. I know what–and who–we're dealing with here."

Before Anderson could offer a reply, he suddenly lost control of the car. "Hey, the wheel's unresponsive," he said, jerking it left and right without any effect.

"Hit the brakes!" Opperman yelled.

Anderson did. Nothing.

"Oh crap!" Anderson said and raised his arms in front of his face. The car careened into a lamp post, ricocheted off at high speed then smashed into an adjacent parked car in a cacophony of wrenching steel and shattering glass.

\* \* \* \* \* \* \*

Leena awoke in the backseat of the Daimler. She blinked a few times, tried to clear her blurred vision. "Max?" she said weakly.

"I'm here. You're safe. We're nearly home."

She felt more pain now than she had ever experienced before in her life. She felt lucky to be alive. The front of her suit was covered in blood, but it appeared otherwise intact, no worse the wear from her ordeal. She wished she could say likewise for her body. Her cowl lay on the seat beside her.

"Max," she said, "let Sloan know about the warehouse. Those weapons mustn't reach their destination."

"Already done," Max replied. She remembered he was used to anticipating such requests.

"Paul had been there at some point recently, but...but..." She couldn't continue.

"We'll find the Chief. I know we will."

Leena let her head sag back onto the headrest. Where was Paul now? She was suffering, exhausted, and felt like an abject failure, like she'd let the city down.

Let Paul down.

She had failed to rescue him. Failed to stop Blackstorm, whomever he was. What had she achieved, if anything? Tears welled in her eyes. She wasn't sure she could keep doing this on her own, but then she realized she had at least been able to determine Paul had been there, and was still alive–in the recent past at any rate. And she felt sure those weapons would now be confiscated and destroyed. She *had* achieved some small measure of success after all. But it wasn't enough, not nearly enough.

And the question remained unanswered–where was Paul now?

# ~ Chapter 8 ~

"What the hell happened to you?" Sloan said.

Opperman opened his eyes. "Where am I?" he whispered.

"You're in the hospital, lucky to be alive. A few abrasions, a concussion, nothing more. Those airbags saved your lives."

"Lives?" He appeared confused.

"Anderson. He has a broken collarbone, some minor whiplash, but he'll be okay as well. He's in the room next door." He pulled up a chair and sat down. "Now, what the hell happened?"

Opperman licked at his dry lips in a vain effort at moistening them. "We lost control of the car. Steering wheel, brakes. Nothing worked."

Sloan rubbed his chin. "We'll get the lab boys to look the car over, but it sounds like sabotage to me."

Opperman attempted to sit upright but immediately fell back onto his pillow. The effort was too much for him.

"Just rest for now. There's nothing more you can do until you're recovered." He stood and started to leave, then stopped. "Oh, before I go...where's the flash drive?"

"I...put it in my pants pocket."

Sloan looked about him and saw a folded pair of trousers over another chair at the far end of the room. He retrieved them and rifled through the pockets. Nothing but lint.

"There's nothing here," Sloan said, anger rising within.

"But...but...I know I put it there," Opperman said, lifting his head slightly from the pillow.

"Damn," Sloan said. "These people seem to be one step ahead of us at every turn."

"The feds," Opperman said softly and plainly, then lay his head back down, closing his eyes.

"Gibbs," Sloan said, more to himself than to Opperman. "I need to speak with Gibbs."

\* \* \* \* \* \* \*

The doorbell rang softly, as though it was old and worn out. Agent Gibbs and a colleague entered the musty corner store, a store that looked like something old Father Time had forgotten about. Thin slivers of sunlight streamed through the grimy windows, illuminating the dust hovering in the air and lying all around them. Clearly this was a store that not many frequented.

As they approached the counter at the far end, a shopkeeper emerged from a backroom and eyed them suspiciously. He was old and appeared as dusty as the rest of the store.

"Anything I can do you for?" he said in a scratchy, decrepit tone.

"I'm Agent Gibbs of the FBI, this is Agent Webber," Gibbs said in rote fashion, flashing his badge. He'd been doing this a long time. "We'd like to ask you a few questions."

"I don't know nuthin'."

Gibbs slapped a photo on the counter, slid it over to the shopkeeper. "I'm told he works here. He in today?"

"Smith? What's he done? I knew I never shoulda hired that punk!" the shopkeeper said. "Once a punk, always a punk."

"Yes, Gerald Smith. Is he here?" Gibbs asked again.

The shopkeeper sighed but quickly acquiesced. "Yeah, he's out back. Readying stock for shelving." He pointed to the door behind him. "You're lucky he's here today. He hardly ever comes to work. But at least he's cheap."

Agent Gibbs and Webber smiled, ignoring the shopkeeper while rounding the counter. They entered the backroom. It was poorly lit, and even grimier than the rest of the store. There in front of them stood a disheveled younger man, placing canned goods and other items on a trolley.

"Gerald Smith," Webber called out.

"Who wants to know?" the man said, not turning.

"FBI," Gibbs said.

"The feds? Whatya want with me."

"Bent Street," Gibbs started.

"Never heard of it," Smith grunted.

"Funny thing, but there's an apartment there you've been seen entering and exiting on numerous occasions," Gibbs said. "We think you worked there."

"So what?"

Webber grabbed Smith and threw him against the trolley. "That was a trap house for children, you sick scumbag."

"Trap...what?" Smith said as Gibbs slapped the cuffs on him.

"Child exploitation. You're going down for the rest of your life," Webber said.

"You have the right to be silent," Gibbs said. "You have the right to an attorney, yadda yadda, blah blah blah."

"Hey!" Smith cried. "You're one of us, huh?" Gibbs and Webber remained silent. "What gives? We're protected. You're supposed to make sure nothing happens to us."

Gibbs grabbed Smith by the arm. "We're beyond that now, mate. The local cops have made an issue of this. It's only a matter of time before the media gets wind of it all and blows this sky high. We need arrests and we need them now."

"But," Smith said, struggling against his bonds, "I was just a low-level groomer. I wasn't actually involved in the...the..."

"We need a fall guy," Webber added, "and you're it. Or at least one of them. Easy to find, easy to patsy. The public will lap it up."

Smith was now in their faces, furious. "I'll talk, I'll tell them you're on the take, everything."

Gibbs smiled broadly. "You do and you won't survive the night. You must know how deep this goes. The people who are behind all this...their reach is everywhere. They can touch–do–anything." Reality dawned upon Smith's face. "You take the fall and we reward you."

"Reward?" Smith said. "What reward?"

"You're allowed to live. Now, stay silent...and live."

Webber took Smith by the other arm and the two agents escorted him from the storeroom.

"You never told me what he did," the storekeeper said as the three appeared from the back.

"Pedophile ring," Webber said. "Real bad character."

The storekeeper was evidently shocked into silence, and the three exited the ramshackle store. Gibbs helped Smith into the back seat of their car.

"You bastards," Smith grumbled under his breath.

"You're welcome," Gibbs replied, taking his position behind the wheel.

\* \* \* \* \* \* \*

Leena lay in her bed, every bone and muscle felt lke they were on fire. Indeed, she could swear her hair follicles were crying out in agony. She had, reluctantly, caught a glance at herself in the bathroom mirror earlier, and instantly regretted it. A broken nose, two black eyes, and lips that looked like she had French-kissed a cheese grater.

She had limped to her bed and hadn't moved an inch since. That was...hours ago? If not, it certainly felt like it. Despite her pain and exhaustion, sleep had thus far eluded her. Her mind was awash with concern for Paul, with feelings of guilt at her inability to save him, with her sense of inadequacy in The Wraith's absence. In truth, deep down, she knew this was all a bunch of hooey, but then the reality of her battered body lying in bed right now brought all those sensitivities back. And this...Blackstorm. On his chest there was a...a cobra. Could this mean...? For the moment, she buried the thought away.

At least one thing had gone right this night. Sloan and his fellow officers had gotten to the warehouse in time. Those weapons would be out of action and quickly disposed of. She felt some small measure of peace at that. And, as much as it galled her to be out of action for the present, she knew full well she needed the rest. She tried again to close her eyes and remove all thoughts from her mind. Sleep would come...eventually.

* * * * * * *

Sloan barged into the interrogation room at Metro Police Plaza, not caring who was inside or what was going on there.

"Detective Sloan," Gibbs said, slightly turning in Sloan's direction. "Agent Webber and I were just having a chat with Mr. Smith here."

Smith sat at the other side of a large table, with Webber seated opposite him and Gibbs standing to their side.

Sloan put his hands on his hips. "Who is he?"

"Oh, just a prime mover in our case. One of the groomers. Trolled the local schools and traveled interstate to do the same there. Gained kids' confidence, then kidnapped them and shipped them here and other locations," Gibbs said.

Smith sat silently, his head bowed.

"We were just taking his statement," Webber added.

"I see," Sloan said. "You're hoping he'll finger those higher up?"

Smith slightly raised an eyebrow at that, Sloan couldn't help but notice, but he said nothing and dropped his head once again.

"I think we should discuss this outside," Gibbs said. "Agent Webber can continue with the interview."

Gibbs led Sloan out in the corridor, closed the door quietly behind them. "What do you think you were doing in there?"

"I was hoping you feds would get some quick results, but this–"

"And we have," Gibbs said. "My men were out canvassing the area, took a number of statements, discovered a series of names from multiple witnesses, and multiple arrests have been made. My men are interviewing a good half dozen perps."

"But they're all surely low-level hoods, paid thugs to do all the dirty work. Not the people we need–"

"Detective Sloan," Gibbs broke in. "I've allowed you into this case as a courtesy, but you're taking things too far now. The FBI is in control here. These suspects are a mix of the high and low. We're taking them out of the child kidnapping business...for good. Now please, we'll take it from here. I don't want to have to speak with your commissioner about this."

This was a brush-off, and Sloan knew it. He also knew it was impossible to get such results, even with just low-level hoods, as quickly as this without having prior knowledge of the situation. Inside knowledge. The thought pained him, but he knew it to be true. And now Gibbs knew that he knew, which put him and his team in even more danger.

On top of that, this would all soon be covered up, with the FBI claiming all the glory at stopping this crime, with the feds no doubt hoping to have Sloan and co. in body bags as the coda to tie it all up nicely.

What to do....Take Harrison into his confidence? Maybe. He also needed to speak with Anderson and Opperman again. Take stock, plan their next move. No matter the situation with the FBI, their prime concern was still this case, and getting justice, true justice, for those poor children.

\* \* \* \* \* \* \*

Sooki closed the hospital door softly behind her. Anderson opened his eyes. He wasn't asleep, just resting, and had heard the door opening and closing.

"How did you know to find me here?"

Tears were welling in Sooki's eyes. Clearly, the sight of Anderson trussed up in his bed affected her greatly. Anderson was touched by this.

"I called your department. Said I was your girl. I heard about the accident on the TV news. I...I was worried."

"Accident? Ha!" Anderson said.

Sooki sat beside him in the room's sole chair. "What are you talking about?"

"The car was tampered with. The wheel went dead, brakes failed, both at once. The car had just been serviced. No way was this a natural mechanical failure."

"What's going on?" Sooki said. She grabbed Anderson's hand and held it firmly.

"It's this case," Anderson said. "We're getting too close for comfort. The feds are involved." He looked at her gravely. "Look, it's not safe to be around me right now. Have you somewhere safe to go? I mean, really safe?"

She nodded.

"Good," Anderson said, smiling. "Then you go there right away and stay there. Don't worry about business. I'll take care of everything. You just go and be safe, okay?"

She nodded again, and stood, then bent over and kissed Anderson gently on the lips.

"Go now," Anderson implored. The sooner she got to safety the better, especially if she was now known to the department, even if only peripherally. He didn't trust anybody. Not anymore. Perhaps Sloan, but...

Sooki left with tears in her eyes. Anderson was conflicted. Was he...in love with her? Was he even capable of such feeling? Perhaps he was. But what of his ambition? His rise within the ranks of his profession. It was something he'd always dreamed of. Indeed, he'd always felt the commissioner's office was his destiny. And, once achieved, what then? The sky was the limit. Perhaps city council, or even the mayor's office? It was all within his grasp. Or was it? Was he just fooling himself? When this was all over, he had a lot to think about.

A knock at the door. "Sooki, I told you–"

Sloan entered before he could finish. "We need to talk."

"Yeah."

"You and Opperman are being targeted. The feds are obviously afraid we're getting somewhere with our investigation. Too close for comfort."

Anderson smirked at those words. He'd just used them with Sooki. A thought suddenly came to him. "But how do they know? On the surface, we really haven't achieved much, if anything. Talked to a few potential witnesses, not much else. Everything that we have uncovered has been unofficial. Nobody but us is aware of it."

Sloan's eyes widened. "You're right. Then..."

"It's an inside job. We have a mole." Anderson paused, pondered the situation over. "There aren't many we've taken into our confidence, but there are enough in-the-know to make the mole's identity unclear at present."

"I'm not so sure about that," Sloan said. "The flash drive is gone."

Anderson couldn't believe what he was hearing. Only the three of them–Sloan, Opperman, and himself–knew of the drive's existence. And Lady Wraith, of course, from whom they had received the device. Anderson wracked his brain.

The thought of Sloan being the mole was unthinkable. He could be a pain in the ass, sure, and had proven to be something of a barrier to his rise up the ranks, but dishonest –crooked–he was not. Likewise for Lady Wraith, not that he knew her personally. But she and her male partner had long proven themselves in the city. That left only one possibility. It, too, was unthinkable, and yet...what did they truly know about Sean Opperman?

"Yeah, I can see what you're thinking," Sloan said. "And I'm thinking the same thing."

Anderson yearned to be up and about. Not only to get back to work, not only to get out there and nail these scum, but he knew he was a sitting duck here in the hospital. "So, whatta we do?"

"I'll get you to a place of safety first," Sloan said. "You're compromised here. I'll do likewise with Opperman on the same pretext, but he'll actually be held under guard. I need to question him first. He can potentially provide us with a lot of answers."

Anderson nodded. He appreciated Sloan now more than ever. Had he been wrong about him all these years? Perhaps so.

"You rest up," Sloan said. "I'll take things from here. I still have a reliable friend in high places I can turn to for help."

\* \* \* \* \* \* \*

Night had fallen and Leena was once again ensconced within the confines of the Lair. She sat at the computer terminal, not doing anything specific. Just thinking. There was always a lot to think about.

The comm-link chimed on her terminal. It was Sloan. She placed the earphones over her head. "Yes, Sloan," she said.

"We've been compromised," Sloan's harried voice came through loud and clear. "We have a traitor in our midst."

He went on to describe the day's events and his ideas on where to take things next. Leena agreed with him and promised to keep in touch with her own investigation, linked as they were to his own.

A whirring of gears, and Max appeared at the upper entrance of the Lair just as Leena signed off with Sloan. Max was quickly by Leena's side.

"Any news?" he said.

"Sloan was right. The feds are trying to cover up everything. Someone's in the back of this. Someone big and powerful, or perhaps many such people, to have such reach. And one of his own men is a part of it all."

Max gasped at that. Corruption within the Metro police force wasn't exactly a rare thing, but the situation had improved in recent years due to the immense efforts of good cops like Harrison and Sloan, as well as those of The Wraith and his team. But this was still shocking.

"What's our next move, then?" Max said.

"Sloan will call if he needs us. As for Paul...I have a meeting scheduled with Patrich Azufi. If you recall, we were interrupted earlier. He has a lot to answer for."

# ~ Chapter 9 ~

"Dammit, dammit, dammit!" Azufi spat into his phone. "Those weapons were worth...how much...a hundred mil? At least. And you're telling me they've been destroyed?" He followed that with several expletives before slamming the phone into its cradle.

He stood from his desk within his office at Latham Industries, rounded it, poured himself a straight Scotch from the crystal decanter on the sideboard and then proceeded to pace back and forth without taking a sip from his glass.

"That idiot Blackstorm better have–"

There was a knocking at the...window? He slowly turned to face the only window in the room, located behind his desk. He was fifty floors up! There was a dark shape there, but who...what?

A compact explosion tore through the glass, sending shards outwards toward Azufi. He instinctively reached his arms up to offer some sort of protection, but was too slow, with several fragments embedding into his cheeks. He screamed in a mixture of terror and pain.

The dark shape burst forth from outside, landing on the desk in a sinister, crouched pose, like some terrifying creature from the worst of nightmares. In seconds, the shape was down and Azufi was in its grip. He could see now who it was–Lady Wraith.

"Where is The Wraith?" she demanded, holding Azufi tightly by the collar.

"B...Blackstorm's got him," he whimpered.

"But why is he being held?"

Azufi merely sputtered some gibberish.

"Why?!"

"I...I thought we could...auction his identity."

"You–what?" Lady Wraith exploded with fury.

"A live unmasking, over the dark web, to the highest bidder."

"Where is he? Where?"

"Blackstorm's got him," Azufi repeated.

"Tell me something I don't know. Where?" She shook him violently.

"I don't know, I don't know. Blackstorm, he's...he's his own guy, you know? He contacts me. I don't know where he is or how to contact him."

Lady Wraith growled and lifted her fist as though to strike him. Azufi closed his eyes, flinched, trembled with fear. He might have even wet his pants. He sobbed. But nothing came. After a few moments of stillness, he braved himself to open his eyes a mere fraction.

Lady Wraith was gone.

\* \* \* \* \* \* \*

Back on the Latham Industries roof, Lady Wraith sat in a heap in the gravel. She breathed deeply, trying to calm herself down. For a moment, just the briefest of moments, she thought she would do Azufi some bodily harm. The anger, the frustration at being so close and still so far, was finally hitting her. Azufi should have known everything, was supposed to...but the reality was, she was still no closer to finding Paul than she had been at the beginning of all this. And that was proving hard for her to take.

*What now? What on Earth do I do now?*

She pondered what her next move would be. Ultimately, only one option came to her. Fatback. She would talk again with Fatty.

\* \* \* \* \* \* \*

"Are you comfortable?"

Sloan was pacing in front of Opperman, who was seated in a chair in a sparsely and dimly lit room.

"What the hell is going on here?" Opperman said. "This is your idea of a safehouse? I saw the armed guard outside."

"And there'll be one in this room shortly," Sloan said.

"What the–?"

"Shut up!" Sloan said. "All I want to hear from you are answers."

"What are you talking about? Are you insane?" Opperman said.

"I know you're on the take," Sloan said. "I know you're working with the feds, I know you've been feeding them information, probably gave them the flash drive, no doubt organized the *accident* with your car."

"You know? You know!" Opperman shrieked. "You know jack shit!"

"I'll take that as a confession."

"You can take it any way you want, you sonuva..."

A knock at the door caused Opperman to stop. An armed officer entered, nodded to Sloan and took a position by the door, the room's only entry.

"What the hell are you thinking?" Opperman shouted. "Do you think you're going to get anywhere? Do you think you're gonna live through this?"

"Is that why you turned?" Sloan said. "The crusader of the Gosch case. Did they threaten you? Or just offer you so much money that you stopped caring about what happens to those kids." He was mad, good and mad. "If I could, I'd tear you apart right now. It's more than you deserve. You know what's happening to those kids right now and will continue to happen. And you're just letting them."

Opperman shot up out of his chair, but Sloan was ready for him, grabbing him by the shoulders and thrusting him back down.

"You're not going anywhere. You're done. It's over. You're only out is to talk. Names, locations. Everything you know...I want it–now!" Sloan cracked the knuckles in his wrists. He truly meant business, and if it took a few lumps in getting it, he would do it.For the kids.

"If I talk, I'm dead. If you bring me in, I'm dead. No real option for me."

"We'll protect you."

Opperman snorted. "Protect me? Don't fool yourself. Look what happened to Epstein. You can't protect me from...him, uh....them..."

"Him? Them?" Sloan noticed the slip. "Who is he? Who are they? Talk and help me bring these bastards to justice. If you're gonna die anyway, as you claim, then let your death mean something." He really didn't care at this point.

Opperman sat in stony silence. Sloan knew what that meant. He'd get nothing out of him. In Opperman's mind, he was dead either way, but silence would perhaps buy his family's or loved one's safety. Sloan knew the spiel.

"With or without your help," Sloan said, leaning down into Opperman's face, "no matter what it takes, I'm gonna make these sick puppies pay. You have my word on that."

He turned and strode for the door. He faced the armed guard. "Look after him. We need him alive to face trial." Sloan held up a hand-held recorder in one hand. "He's going down, but one way or the other, he's going to spill his guts and take the rest of them with him."

\* \* \* \* \* \* \*

"What do you want with me now?"

Fatback and Lady Wraith were meeting again in the same alley as before. It was just as cold, just as late, and Fatback was clearly just as annoyed.

"You know what I want," Lady Wraith said. "Information."

"I ain't got none."

"You know everything that goes on in this town," Lady Wraith said, striking a menacing tone. "I bet you can tell me all about Blackstorm."

Fatback's demeanor changed instantly upon hearing the name. He knew damn well who he was, Lady Wraith thought.

"I see you recognize that name," Lady Wraith said. "You're clearly frightened by its mere mention. Who is he? Where is he holding The Wraith?"

"I...I don't know. I...I can't say."

"Which is it, Fatty?"

"Don't call me that," Fatback said.

"Answers, Fatty...now!" Lady Wraith growled. This constant to-ing and fro-ing was really starting to infuriate her.

She was in his face now, teeth bared, fury emanating from her every pore. "Look, I don't know who he is. Not really."

"Then tell me what you *do* know."

"All right, all right. He's from overseas, the Middle East they say. An emissary of someone called the Cobra. I don't know this guy, but that's the word on the street."

Lady Wraith couldn't help but gasp at the mention of the Cobra's name. She had no time to try and make sense of it.

"Where can I find him?" Lady Wraith demanded.

"I...I..."

"I'm getting tired of your stalling," Lady Wraith said, grabbing Fatback by the collar. "Tell me now or I *will* hurt you."

"The waterfront...near the Christopher Docks," Fatback said. "He rarely ventures far from home base."

"Specifics!" Lady Wraith growled again.

"Stake the area out, you'll soon find the place."

With a grunt, Lady Wraith threw Fatback harshly into the wall to her left. He hit the brick roughly and landed awkwardly.

"That the thanks I get?" Fatback called out.

But Lady Wraith barely heard him.

# ~ Chapter 10 ~

Sloan strode toward through the lengthy hallway toward the squad room where his desk was located at police headquarters. Agent Gibbs emerged from a side door, saw Sloan, and blocked his progress. They were alone and Gibbs didn't look happy.

"I'm glad I bumped into you. We need to talk," Gibbs said, clearly agitated.

"Don't you have someone else to frame?" Sloan said, probably with a more barbed tone than he perhaps should have used.

"I'm getting pretty tired of you, Sloan."

"Likewise," Sloan said. "Whatya gonna do about it?"

Gibbs leaned in close in an attempt to intimidate him. Sloan had been accosted by bigger–and better–men than him. He smirked at Gibbs.

"Take your big tough guy routine elsewhere," Sloan said. "I'm not some rookie constable you can just push around."

Gibbs leaned back. "When I'm through with you, you'll be lucky to still make constable. You're more likely to be cleaning the latrines at the academy...if they'll have you."

That got Sloan's gander up. What with everything going on, trying desperately to help those poor children, then dealing with crooked cops and FBI agents, The Wraith missing, and now some new super villain making his presence felt in the city. Now this dirty agent was giving him lip. It was too much. Sloan let loose with a right hand to the jaw. Gibbs never saw it coming. He never saw the floor either, barreling down into it.

"I'll have your badge for this, Sloan," Gibbs said while getting to his knees. He rubbed his jaw gingerly.

"What's going on here?" Commissioner Harrison boomed as he exited his office and saw the two of them further along the hallway.

Gibbs stood, made to say something, then held back. He smiled. "Nothing, sir, I just slipped here. Detective Sloan was about to help me up."

"Mm hmm," Harrison said with a raised eyebrow. Sloan knew he wasn't buying it, but what else could he do under the circumstances.

"Any disagreements here, take it outside," Harrison said. "Or better yet, get on with your duties like real professionals. This isn't some silly schoolyard."

Gibbs nodded and mock saluted him. Harrison eyed Sloan intently, but said nothing more and walked away.

Alone again, Sloan didn't know what to make of this. Gibbs smiled mischievously. "Breaking you officially is no longer enough. I'm going to hurt you. And more. Much more," Gibbs said in a low but harsh tone.

"Bring it on, pussy," Sloan goaded him. "I'll be waiting for you." He blew the agent a kiss.

Gibbs smirked and walked away in the same direction as Harrison. Sloan was alone. He took a deep breath. For all his bravado, he was no fool, and knew the grave danger he was in, his wife was in, now more than ever. He had to take stock, plan his next move, and he hoped against hope that, somehow, Opperman would come to his senses and turn State's evidence.

Yeah, and Hell would freeze over.

* * * * * * *

The waterfront by the Christopher Docks, especially at such a late hour, almost seemed like another world. Long since abandoned as the city's entry point to the world for a position further upriver in deeper waters, the area had since become a desolate part of the city filled with the desolate and criminal.

Lady Wraith was positioned in a prime spot atop a deserted warehouse–one of many such structures which littered the precinct–hugging a crumbling brick smokestack. She scanned her surrounds with her night-vision lenses.

"Nothing here so far," Lady Wraith said into her comm-link, "apart from the usual flotsam that resides here."

"I've not seen anything untoward either," Max said through the link. "Not unless you count a couple of homeless people getting amorous in the alley close to my position."

Lady Wraith found that to be both humorous and sadly appalling at the same time. She wondered briefly if, perhaps, Fatback was trying to lead her astray...but then dismissed the notion. He wouldn't dare, she thought. He was too much of a coward. She settled back down for a long, monotonous vigil.

She only hoped it would prove a fruitful one.

\* \* \* \* \* \* \*

Sloan sat at his desk, morose and silent. This case, and all its permutations, was finally really getting to him. The implications were enormous, and there were very few people he could turn to. He felt alone and, just a little, frightened. He slapped his fist down onto his desk. He hated feeling this way, hated having his emotions compromised thus. He prided himself in being a bad-ass, an old-fashioned man's man, someone who took no prisoners and shed no tears. Deep down, though, he was a bit of a softie...he just didn't let anyone know that.

He gazed wistfully and his partner's desk across from him. Perez was one of the few that knew him–the real him–all too well, and he was proud that she did. He hoped she was not only doing well, but would also get back to work quickly. He needed her now more than ever, more than he even thought possible.

He forced his thoughts back to the case. Opperman's slip of the tongue was telling. *Him,* which became *them,* in quick succession. What did it mean? Which was truly accurate? Or were both true? Who was *he* and *they*? It had to be someone of immense wealth and power. That realization did nothing to narrow down the field. How many multi-millionaires and billionaires lived in the US alone? Too many to count. Even Metro City had its fair share of snouts in the trough. Opperman's slip really didn't amount to all that much. He needed to know more, but how? Opperman wasn't talking, would likely never talk, shy of resorting to actual torture. Was there a way he could trick Opperman into spilling his guts? The thought intrigued Sloan. It sounded promising. Something to mull over, certainly. Perhaps Anderson would have an idea.

The phone rang, stirring him from his mental contortions. "Sloan here. Yes?" His heart quickly sank. "No, how is this possible? There were multiple guards stationed." This was proving to be a nightmare. "Outside help? For Pete's sake, I'll be right there." He paused to take it all in. "Dammit!" Sloan slammed the phone back into its cradle.

Things were going from bad to worse. Opperman had escaped. But that wasn't quite accurate. He'd been *broken free*. Armed assailants had appeared, murdered the guards–good cops one and all–and had quickly extricated Opperman from his safehouse. Clearly, they had known the location of the safehouse, known the details of Opperman's situation. An inside job. Gibbs. Rage filled every pore of his being in that moment, but Sloan knew he had to contain it, use it, funnel it into the right direction–nailing those responsible.

He grabbed his coat and headed for the exit. He had to get to the safehouse as quickly as possible.

\* \* \* \* \* \* \*

The night moved slowly for Lady Wraith. She kept to her vigil diligently, remained on the alert for any sign of Blackstorm, or anything out of the ordinary that might indicate something was amiss. But there was nothing. Nothing at all. She was starting to worry. It was closing in on six weeks without Paul. Six weeks where anything might have happened to him. The thought of something happening to Paul, something serious, sickened her. She had to stop herself from sinking into a morass of doom and gloom. But it was difficult and proving to be more difficult with each passing day. And that, too, was worrying her.

Then, something caught the corner of her eye. She tapped at a spot on her temple, activating the zoom lenses within her night-vision. There appeared to be some concentrated activity at the entrance to a narrow alleyway down on street level a few blocks away. It could be anything. A drug deal, some sort of gang meeting, any number of other illicit conducts. Or it could be something connected with Paul's disappearance. Either way, it bore looking into.

"There might be something going on here off Plough Street," Lady Wraith said into her comm-link. "I'm heading down to take a look."

"Be careful," Max quickly replied over the link.

\* \* \* \* \* \* \*

Sloan arrived at the safehouse to find a platoon of local cops there. The place looked as though a battalion of the marine corps had come storming through it. The bodies of his fallen officers were still on the ground outside and within. Forensic officers milled about, and the street was cordoned off.

*This much firepower, this much effort, for just one man,* Sloan thought. *Opperman clearly knows much. Whoever's back of all this was obviously afraid Opperman would talk. I'm surprised they didn't just knock him off at the same time then.*

That last thought registered with Sloan. It suddenly made sense to him Opperman was rescued by people he knew, people that likely were his friend or friends. The FBI? Gibbs?

"Detective Sloan," a middle-aged, stocky Latino plain-clothed officer said, approaching him.

"Yes," Sloan said. "And you are?"

"Detective Jimenez, Fourth Precinct. I'm told this location was being used as a safehouse containing a suspect of yours."

"That's right. Sorry to see all this–"

"Next time," Jimenez interrupted, clearly agitated, "alert those in this precinct of your plans and we can work together on this. Maybe prevent such an outcome from occurring. Some professional courtesy wouldn't have gone amiss."

That got Sloan's gander up. "Correct me if I'm wrong– *Jimenez*–but the point of a safehouse is to keep knowledge of its existence to as few people as possible. I don't know you or anyone else in your precinct from a bar of soap. Trust is more important to me than courtesy."

Jimenez smirked. "Someone obviously knew about this place anyway."

Sloan got right into Jimenez's face, their noses practically squashed together. Both were similar in age, but Sloan had half a head on him in height and several more pounds in muscle. "Get away from me, buster, or I may do something I will regret."

Jimenez initially appeared to want to stand his ground, perhaps not give an inch to his opposite number, but seemed to quickly think better of it. Sloan was in no mood for courtesies right now. Jimenez smiled weakly then retreated, disappearing into the milling throng of officers.

Back alone with his thoughts, Sloan returned to the topic at hand.

*Yeah. Gibbs! It all comes back to that scumbag.*

He went over to each of the bodies of his fallen comrades and bade them farewell with a silent prayer. He felt responsible, in a way, for their demise, but knew those that were truly responsible were still out there. And he would find them. Of that he had no doubt.

\* \* \* \* \* \* \*

Lady Wraith had reached the alleyway off Plough Street only minutes later, but found it deserted. The group of around five to ten men that she had witnessed were gone.

*Where could they be?*

The alley was narrow, almost completely shrouded in darkness, and strewn with a myriad of garbage and what appeared to be several homeless people fast asleep. At least she hoped they were.

She had a bad feeling about this, but ultimately there was no other option but to continue down the precarious, snowy path. With her night-vision lenses, it was no problem navigating her way, but the hairs on the back of her neck were standing on end. This felt like a trap. And yet...

Finally, she found herself within the adjacent building. She quickly switched off her night-vision. What appeared from the outside as nothing more than a dilapidated pile was anything but on the inside. It was a large warehouse-style room, well-lit, the walls and floor all bathed in a cream color scheme. There was no furniture, there was no sign of anyone about. Except...

"Greetings," Blackstorm said at the far end of the room. He stood there facing her. Defiant, ready for battle. "I see you found your way here to me. Just as I had planned."

Lady Wraith knew she was in trouble. Deep trouble.

## ~ Chapter 11 ~

*Fatty! That bastard set me up.*

Blackstorm loomed before Lady Wraith, his form large and threatening. He was clearly itching for a fight, and she wasn't sure she was ready for another tumble with him.

"It was so easy to lure you here," Blackstorm said. "I fail to see the threat you and this Wraith are to my master. Neither of you have any power over me."

A reference to his master. The logo on his chest. The implications made Lady Wraith shudder. She hoped against hope he was merely toying with her, that it wasn't possible for the Cobra to still be alive. Because he couldn't be. He couldn't.

"Where is The Wraith?" Lady Wraith said, trying to shake her fears from her mind.

"He is here, of course," Blackstorm said.

She wasn't sure whether to believe him or not. "Show him to me."

"The only way to see him, the only way to free him, is through me. You must best me, or his fate is sealed." He tensed his muscles. He was ready.

She was sure he was lying, but one thing was true. She had to get through him to get to Paul. That much was clear. She remembered the beating he had given her at their last encounter. She was still sore. She wasn't sure she was yet ready for a rematch. But there appeared to be no other choice. She had to approach this differently. Use her brains. She could outsmart this guy. She had to try.

"Come, let me finish you quickly," Blackstorm said. "I will make this as painless as possible." He positioned himself in a battle stance. It was now or never.

Lady Wraith cried out like a warrior of old–and charged. Blackstorm allowed her to come to him, and lashed out, connecting with her jaw, sending her plummeting to the ground. She rubbed her jaw, hoped against hope it wasn't broken. Bravado was not enough.

*Think, Leena, think. Charging at him like a rogue bull isn't exactly outsmarting him.*

Blackstorm remained still, waiting for her stand and commit again to battle. He was no doubt waiting for her to slip up, and then would move in for the kill.

*Not this time, Mister.*

She stood, a little shakily at first, then reached into her belt, produced a small handful of smoke pellets, and lobbed them at her opponent's feet. In seconds, he was completely obscured by a thick, pungent fog. She heard him hacking and flailing about, and felt encouraged she had been able to catch him unawares. She knew she had to press the advantage. Use whatever she had to try and overpower him. Flash powder wasn't an option, and neither were her makeshift Eyes of Judgment. She needed Blackstorm alive, or perhaps all would be lost. She had to give him the beating of his life and hope that would be enough.

She lashed out with blow after blow, connecting with powerful lefts and rights. A kick to the groin, a knee to the face, a spinning kick to the head. Using her adrenalin to her benefit, she let loose with all the strength she had and then some. With the smoke clearing, she didn't dare tarry, and continued with the barrage, not allowing Blackstorm the ability to defend, let alone fight back. He tried to regain the upper hand, but was clearly weakening. Perhaps he had never received such a pummeling before.

With the villain on his knees, she continued slamming him with her fists. He was taking it, but Lady Wraith saw he was beginning to sag under the weight of her brutal attack. Again and again she lashed out. Again and again Blackstorm withstood each savage blow. Every attempt at a punch of his own either missed its mark or was now easily blocked. The tide had turned. Until, at last, he teetered...and fell.

For a few moments, Lady Wraith remained rooted to the spot, not yet willing to believe the battle was over. That she had won. Perhaps Blackstorm was merely feigning unconsciousness. That was surely his sort of game. Maybe he was about to strike violently, and it would all be over quickly. But he did not move. She finally allowed herself to move and check his prone body. He was alive, but out cold.

She stood and, briefly, wasn't sure what to do with herself, then quickly snapped back to attention. Paul. She had to check if he was, indeed, in situ. There were only two doors in this place: the one she had entered by, and another behind where Blackstorm originally stood. She sprinted for it, passed through into a smaller, shabbier room. And there, up against the chipping brick wall, was The Wraith. Shackled. His arms were manacled at the wrist, the chains reaching up and attaching at a point in the moldy ceiling. His ankles were similarly chained to the wooden floor. He was unconscious and sagged against his bonds.

"Darling," Lady Wraith cried upon seeing him. She lunged for him, checked his pulse. It was racing, but he was alive. He wasn't unconscious per se, more drugged, his dilated pupils clear evidence of it. Heaven only knew what this might have done to him.

Quickly, not wishing to wait another moment, she used a laser cutter from her belt to free him, then placed a shoulder of his over hers, and began to drag him toward the exit. He started to mumble something incoherent, but she knew he was not really awake. She had to get him to safety before...

Upon reaching the main hall, Blackstorm was standing once more. Even after taking such a beating, he had recovered quickly and now appeared prepared to start the fight all over again. She doubted she had the energy or strength for another go-round.

"I have been bested," Blackstorm said, "by a female. I have been embarrassed and have brought shame upon my master. This I cannot brook. Neither can my master allow such. I have failed him. My fate is sealed."

A moment of silence, then an audible crack broke the momentary silence. Blackstorm began to sway on his feet. He gurgled, then toppled with a smack on the wooden floor. His body jerked once, then twice, an exhalation, then nothing. Even at her distance from him, she knew Blackstorm was dead, had taken his own life rather than live with the shame of having been beaten by a woman, nor was he willing to have–the Cobra?–deal him the death blow. He obviously felt this was his only alternative. And took it.

Lady Wraith wasn't willing to give the matter another thought. She had Paul back safely. That's all that counted right now.

"Max," she said into her comm-link. "Emergency evac. Track my whereabouts and meet me on Plough Street."

And, with great difficulty, she exited the building, with the motionless body of her fiancé in tow.

\* \* \* \* \* \* \*

It was early morning. Agent Gibbs exited Metro Police Plaza with a skip in his step and made his way down the stairs toward the sidewalk. He appeared chirpy, whistled a tune as he strode downtown, not making his way to his car as Sloan thought he would.

Sloan was across the street, seated discreetly in his car. He watched Gibbs walking away intently. He knew that whatever answers there were in this case, they lay with Gibbs. So far, he was the focal point for everything that had transpired. Either way, he knew something, likely something big, and Sloan was no longer willing to play by the book. Far from it.

Down the street some ways, Sloan spotted Gibbs hopping into the backseat of a grey C-Class Mercedes sedan. As the luxury car inched out into traffic, Sloan did likewise with his beat-up Continental. He kept his car a safe distance back, which wasn't hard in any typical Metro thoroughfare, but managed to never lose sight of his quarry up ahead. The Mercedes took a few turns into adjacent side streets but kept to its path within Metro's bustling downtown district.

Sloan doggedly kept on Gibbs' trail. Ultimately, the Mercedes left downtown and glided effortlessly into the inner boroughs. Businesses and stores gave way to row upon row of brownstone homes. Some in decent to good condition, many not. Continuing to maintain a discreet distance, Sloan wondered how long this journey would take. He quickly scanned his Timex wristwatch. It was almost an hour already. He sighed and continued his pursuit.

At last, the dark Merecedes came to a halt in front of a three-storey brownstone, typical of the area, not appearing to be anything other than a middle-class home within easy commute to the city's business district. Gibbs exited the car and hurriedly skipped up the steps to the door. A knock, and it opened, and inside the agent slipped with ease.

Sloan parked the car nearby and eyed the abode intently. There was nothing to suggest it was anything other than a home. But, in researching Gibbs' background, Sloan found this was not where the agent lived, nor could he find any suggestion of relatives living in this area. Friends? Perhaps, but Sloan thought it much more likely to be friends of a different sort. Either way, he wasn't letting Gibbs out of his sight. Not anymore.

He crossed the street carefully and ambled toward the brownstone in question. A laneway ran alongside it out toward its rear, which Sloan traversed, making sure not to be seen by anyone still within the parked car out front. A high wooden fence surrounded the home's side and rear. There were no windows on the side, but plenty out back. Running down the house's side was a drainpipe. It appeared sturdy enough. Checking about him, Sloan nimbly clambered up and over the fence and then started to do likewise up the drainpipe. It was tough going, and difficult to keep the noise levels to a minimum, but he managed to reach the roof with some effort.

It was treacherous up here. The rooftiles were slippery and the butterfly shape to the roof didn't help the matter any. Picking his way along very carefully, Sloan peered over the edge down toward the front street. The Mercedes was still there, but from his current angle, the driver was hidden from view. There was a skylight over to his right, and Sloan inched his way over to it. It was domed upward and made of obscure glass. He listened carefully but heard nothing. Sloan gripped it and pulled. He found, to his immense joy, it was unlatched. Judiciously, he crawled inside and found himself in what appeared to be an attic, or some sort of storage area. In amongst a myriad of boxes, he trod cautiously and silently. At the far end was a folded ladder, and he knew this was the downward exit. Dare he use it? Again, he heard nothing, so he carefully opened the door and lowered the ladder.

Sloan quickly relatched the door and scanned his surroundings. He was on an upper landing. The lighting was low, and there appeared to be no one about. He heard nothing. Narrow stairs leading down were the only direction he could take, and he followed that path slowly.

On the floor below, the lighting was better, and he thought he could hear faint voices coming from somewhere nearby. Noting its direction, he made his way down there carefully, along a lengthy corridor, hoping against hope he could remain undetected. At the far end, round a small bend, was a closed door. Voices emanated from it. He placed an ear to the door. He could hear Gibbs talking to...whom? Was it...Opperman?

"Thanks for getting me outta there," Opperman said.

"You're lucky to still be alive," Gibbs said sharply, clearly not happy being there. "If I had my way, my guys would have blown you away like the they did the cops."

"You bastard," Opperman said under his breath.

"My wishes were overruled," Gibbs said. "From the Head himself."

Sloan heard a gasp; he figured most likely from Opperman. "But...but..."

"Yes," Gibbs said, "you heard right. He's alive, still in control of...well, everything, really."

"Look, Gibbs..." Opperman said nervously, "I didn't talk. I swear I didn't. You know me, I'm not stupid."

"I know you're not, Sean," Gibbs said as smooth and calm as anyone ever spoke.

"Then let me loose, will ya?" Opperman pleaded. "You can trust me."

There was a silent pause. Sloan wondered what was going on. He wished he could see into the room as well as he could hear things.

"No, Sean, I don't think so. You see, the Head didn't allow me to terminate you–at least not yet–but he does want to know whether you squealed or not."

"But I just told you–" Opperman blurted.

"Yes, but you see, Sean...the Head doesn't know you as well as I do. He wants to know for sure whether he has to take further...remedial action. You see, he'd rather not be forced to take down a sizeable portion of Metro City's finest unless he truly has to. Such action would create a lot of headlines he'd prefer to avoid. That's why you're here."

"I didn't talk, I swear it. Sloan and his team don't know anything," Opperman said.

"They know you're corrupt," Gibbs said. "That alone is a little too much knowledge. But we're getting a little ahead of ourselves here. Relax, Sean. You'll be fine. I'm not someone prone to violence, after all. Mr. Walker and Mr. Smith here will take good care of you. I promise, there will be no pain."

The sounds of a scuffle–perhaps that of a man struggling to free himself from his bonds–was heard.

"Now, now, Sean," Gibbs said softly. "Fighting this will only cause you pain. I don't want that. You don't want that. Just relax. It'll all be over soon."

"Get that needle away from me," Opperman spat.

*Needle...Sodium Pentothal most likely*, Sloan thought.

"There, that didn't hurt did it?" Gibbs said after the sounds of further resisting had ceased. "Just relax, take some deep breaths. I just have a few questions for you, then you'll be left in peace."

A few moments of silence.

"Looks like he's calmed down some," another voice said.

"Yes, the effects of the drug are beginning to take hold," Gibbs said. "He should be able to answer now. Sean...Sean, can you hear me?"

"Yes," Opperman replied in a soft, monotone voice.

"Good," Gibbs said. "Let's start then, shall we? What does Sloan know about our...operations here?"

"He knows I'm involved. He knows about the drugs and weapons. He knows some big names are implicated and–"

"W...wait there," Gibbs said. "What was that you said?"

"He knows there are some big names involved, but I destroyed his list before he had a chance to peruse it," Opperman countered.

There was a pause. Sloan could well imagine Gibbs thinking long and hard about what he'd just heard.

"Are you sure of that?"

"I..." Opperman said. "I think so. Sloan handed me the USB drive before he could take a look at its contents."

"But are you sure of that?" Gibbs shouted.

"I...I'm not completely sure."

A loud smack emanated from the room, perhaps Gibbs venting his frustration on a prone and helpless Opperman.

"It's as I feared," Gibbs said. "And where did Sloan obtain this information?"

"From Lady Wraith."

Silence. Sloan straightened, tried to iron out the kinks in his back. His mind was awhirl with all he had heard. And who was this "Head" Gibbs kept referring to? Obviously the one pulling the strings, obviously the one whom everyone was afraid of, the one who had the dope on everything and everyone. But who was he?

"Then you're of no further use to us," Gibbs suddenly said.

Gunfire exploded from the room. Two shots were fired.

"Holy shit!" Sloan said.

Speedy footfalls were heard approaching the door. Sloan cursed himself–he had given himself away. He turned and ran the way he had come. The door opened behind him.

"Sloan!" Gibbs cried out. "Get him."

Not on your life.

Sloan ran faster than he ever had in his life. He reached the door leading to the attic and quickly climbed the ladder. He managed to secure the door from the inside to buy himself some time, then made his way up onto the roof and down the drainpipe.

He plonked down into the side alley, but knew Gibbs and his cronies would soon be on his tail again. Not wishing to run out into the main street yet, where his car was parked and where he would no doubt be easily spotted, he sprinted in the opposite direction, into a rear lane, then across and down a side street. He hailed a passing cab and, soon, was off back to the city. As far as he could tell, he wasn't sighted since the upper landing back in the brownstone. He was glad of that. He was now able to at least catch his breath.

*Opperman's gone, and I was nearly next. But what have I really learned here? Nothing much. Suspicions confirmed, but that's all. And where do I go from here?*

It was a conundrum that troubled Sloan all the way back to the city.

\* \* \* \* \* \* \*

Leena sat beside Paul as he lay in their bed back at home, stroking his forehead and cheek. He was still unconscious and, by his standards at least, painfully thin. He was likely drugged most of the time he was imprisoned, and thus ate very little, if anything at all. His wrists were red and blue and bloody, evidence of being shackled for some considerable time. Her heart ached for him, but at least he was now home and safe. She only hoped and prayed he would soon wake and prove himself to be truly all right.

"Leena," Max said softly.

Leena turned to face the Irishman, who was now standing in the open doorway of the master bedroom.

"You need to eat, get some rest," Max said.

"No," she said, "not until I know he's okay."

"You heard Doc Needham," Max said. "The Chief will likely be out 'til morning with all those drugs in his system. Even with his metabolism, it won't be sooner than that."

"Whenever he wakes, I'll be here. End of story."

"Okay, have it your way," Max said. "I'll have Simpson send something up for you."

He disappeared without a reply from her.

She returned her gaze to her fiancé. He was home and safe, that much was true, but until he opened his eyes and told her he was okay, she couldn't breathe easy. No matter what it took, she would wait.

And hope for the best.

# ~ Chapter 12 ~

"**N**o way," Anderson said.

Sloan sat opposite him in the safehouse he had arranged for his colleague. Anderson appeared well and had around-the-clock care from a live-in nurse who sat nearby.

"I can't go back home. I did manage to get my wife to safety," Sloan said, "but I really don't know where to go next with this."

"We're in a jam, that's for sure," Anderson said. "I'm just sorry I can't do more for you right now. I hate being sidelined like this."

"Never mind," Sloan said. "You just get better. Concentrate on that. I just wanted to keep you informed, is all."

"I appreciate that," Anderson said with a sigh.

"Dammit," Sloan said. "We're no closer now than we were before. And we're hemmed in here. Helpless to do anything without any evidence." He was frustrated and at a loss on how to proceed.

"Wait," Anderson chimed in. "Lady Wraith. Surely she still has the files? Surely she wouldn't have given you the master copy?"

Sloan's demeanor instantly changed. Why hadn't he thought of that? "Dammit, Anderson, you're right. We might still be able to blow this case wide open after all." He stood and pulled his cell phone from his pocket. He pressed a button on it and smiled. "Rest up here. I'll keep you in the loop. Wish me luck."

Before he could get an answer, he was out the door and off.

\* \* \* \* \* \* \*

The late afternoon sun streamed into the master bedroom at Sanderson House. Leena was in a daze and was only peripherally aware of the glare being cast all around her.

"Turn off that light." Leena heard a murmur.

"Paul," she cried, snapping to attention. She turned to him, still lying on the bed, but his eyes were now flickering open. "You're home safe."

"Water," he gasped, and Leena swiftly poured him a glass from a carafe on her bedside chest. She gently held it to his lips. He drank freely.

"Not too fast," Leena said. "There. How do you feel?"

Paul blinked his eyes fully open, smiled weakly at her. "Weak. Thirsty. Hungry."

Leena smiled. They were all good signs. She felt more assured of his recovery and could finally allow herself the luxury of breathing a little easier. "I'll take care of everything. Some rest and you'll be as good as new."

Paul eyed her with a look of serious concern. Leena well knew that look. "The children, Leena. We have to help those children."

She was well aware of what Paul was referring to, but she needed him to rest, recover. Goodness only knew what Blackstorm had done to him while he was incarcerated. "Paul, please. It's being taken care of, I've—"

"No, Leena. Nothing else matters," Paul said, sitting upright and almost looking like he would get out of bed and march away. He seemed to stop himself, however. "Those children. I was locked away with them for a time at the house on Bent Street—"

"Yes, I know. You left your initials there as a clue for me..." Leena began.

"Yes, but...Leena, I know where they're taking the children. Don't you see? Before it's too late. They were taken to a hangar at the Lidstone Airport, waiting for distribution around the country."

Leena's eyes widened in horror. Those poor children. Paul was right. She had to take action. She had to rescue those poor innocents. In this very moment, nothing else mattered. "Rest. Leave it all with me."

She strode from the bedroom without another thought.

She practically ran downstairs, across the foyer and into the library. With the push of a button, she rushed into the Lair and made her way down the gantry toward her cache of Lady Wraith suits. Max was already there, tinkering away in his workshop as he often did. He looked up at Leena as she sped through the Lair.

"You're in a hurry," he said.

The communication's terminal buzzed an incoming call. Max raced there.

"Sloan's on the line," he said.

Leena was there a few seconds later to answer. "Yes, Sloan." She paused to listen. "Meet me in the alley near the entrance to Montgomery Street. We have much to discuss and little time to do so."

She sat at the computer and downloaded a series of data onto a USB stick.

"What's the situation?" Max said, watching Leena work.

"Sloan's lost the USB drive. I'm bringing him the files again. And Paul supplied some intel as to the children's location here in Metro City."

"The Chief," Max said, clearly surprised Paul had not only awoken but had provided such vital information. "The children? From the trap house?"

"On Bent Street, yes. They're in a hangar at the airport in Lidstone. We have to hurry."

"Suit up," Max said. "I'll get the car ready."

* * * * * * *

Sloan was already in the alley when Lady Wraith arrived. The sun had only just set, and a biting cold had quickly settled in. Snow still lay on the streets, and Sloan warmed himself by rubbing his shoulders then his hands together.

"Sloan," Lady Wraith said, standing behind him.

He whirled, not knowing she had been there. "Geez!" He recovered his composure quickly. "Thanks for meeting me."

"Here," Lady Wraith said, handing him another USB stick. "Don't lose it this time."

"I won't."

"There are a lot of names there. Many of them local, many you wouldn't expect."

Sloan nodded grimly.

"Get to work on that. Make the arrests, clean this mess up as best you can," Lady Wraith said.

"What will you do?" Sloan said.

"The children from Bent Street...I'm going to save them."

# ~ Chapter 13 ~

Sloan barged into Commissioner Harrison's office. He was working late, as he usually did, but he clearly didn't appreciate the interruption.

"What the...? Sloan! Have you forgotten how to knock?" Harrison muttered.

Sloan ignored the jibe, held up the USB stick. "I have evidence here. The pedophile ring. Names, details, you name it."

"Dare I ask where you obtained this?" Harrison said, his eyes narrowing.

"Anonymous source," Sloan said.

"Mm hm," Harrison said, not taking the issue any further. "Let's see what we have here, then."

He took the stick from Sloan and indicated for his subordinate to sit alongside him. Harrison plugged the USB into his computer and opened the drive. As Sloan had said, there were names there, details of the kinds of children the names preferred, dates and locations, even some photos. It was all sickening to look at, but it was the evidence they needed. Sloan read through it all. Even Gibbs and Opperman were named, not as abusers, but as those officials who were assigned to protect the guilty. At any cost. No mention of the identity of the Head, however, the one whom Gibbs had mentioned, but there was plenty there to end this ring once and for all.

"I see Sean Opperman named here," Harrison said. "He won't see the back of any prison cell. His body was found just an hour or so ago, fished out of the harbor. From what I was told, it looked like a shark, or some such creature, had taken some hefty chunks out of him."

Sloan wasn't surprised to hear that. He'd been there when his erstwhile colleague had been murdered. "Where's Gibbs and the rest of his bunch?"

"I haven't seen them around today," Harrison said. "They'd likely be home now."

Sloan wondered at that. He stood, exited the office, and walked down the hallway into the squad room. A middle-aged female cop strode by.

"Johnson," Sloan called to her. "Have you seen Agent Gibbs or any of his team today?"

"Not today, no," Johnson said. "Not since early yesterday. Have you checked their office? Maybe they're working late?"

By then, Harrison had joined Sloan and followed him back down the hallway into the office Gibbs and his men had been using. Harrison plunged into the room. It was empty. Not just empty...but cleaned out. No paperwork, no computers, nothing. Not even dust.

"Aw hell," Sloan said.

They'd been too late. Rather than go on the offensive, as Sloan had feared and expected, they had gone the opposite route and fled. Perhaps they knew taking Sloan and any other good cop out was too much for them, would cause too much publicity? Whatever the reason, Agent Gibbs and his team were gone.

"Put out an APB on those punks," Harrison said. "No matter what pull they have, what connections, I want them found. I want them brought to justice. Is that understood?"

"Yes, sir," Sloan said.

"And arrange some warrants," Harrison continued. "We're gonna be busy tonight."

\* \* \* \* \* \* \*

Lady Wraith stood atop a huge shipping crate in a field beside the Lidstone Airport. It was not Metro's major international airport Melton Memorial; it was not much of an airport at all, but a small field which, occasionally, handled certain domestic traffic when Melton had reached capacity. She scanned the tarmac with her zoom night-vision lenses. A blustery, bitterly cold wind curled around and through her. A plane came into view, approaching from the west.

"Charter plane," Lady Wraith said into her comm-link.

"Not listed on any official manifest," Max replied over the link.

"Looks like we got here just in time," Lady Wraith said. "Get ready to move in."

As it came in for a landing, some vans screeched onto the runway from the right-hand side and parked. Lady Wraith watched on intently. Several people exited the vans, and Lady Wraith instantly recognized one of them—Agent Gibbs. His team followed him as they approached the rear of the now stationary plane. The side of the plane was emblazoned with the logo for Metro City Hands, a local Catholic charity. The reality of what was about to happen revolted her.

"Max, it's the feds. Gibbs and his crew."

A large ramp at the rear of the aircraft lowered and a muscular form soon emerged. As he rounded the plane, coming into full view, Lady Wraith couldn't help but gasp.

"No...it's not possible," she said.

"What is it? Report." Max sounded concerned.

"Quickly, Max, move in," Lady Wraith said, regaining her composure. "They'll soon be preparing to board. Get the kids away now!"

Lady Wraith had to act quickly. She had to give Max enough time to get to the children and to evacuate them safely while she dealt with the group on the runway. Any further delay could cost lives. She reached for the grapnel in her belt, fired a line up toward the nearest power pole, and swung out toward the airstrip.

Her cape spread like a mythical vampiric creature of the night and Lady Wraith ballooned up and over her quarry, crashing down between Gibbs and his agents and the man who had exited the plane—Blackstorm.

"Evildoers," Lady Wraith said upon landing. "Your time has come. Now you will face judgment for your sins."

Agent Gibbs and another of his men raised their pistols, ready to fire as soon as they could, but Lady Wraith beat them to the punch. She lobbed several smoke pellets down at their feet, engulfing them in a thick, pungent haze. Into it she plunged, lashing out at anyone that stood. In a flurry of movement, she dispatched with each FBI agent in turn, connecting with powerful blows to the face and body with

LADY WRAITH | 117

fists and feet. She was in no mood for anything but violent action.

As the smoke cleared, each agent lay on the asphalt, unconscious and disarmed, though Lady Wraith could not spot Gibbs amongst them.

"I have been looking forward to such a challenge," Blackstorm said, having watched the battle from the end of the plane's ramp. "Come, let us see this to the end."

\* \* \* \* \* \* \*

Max gunned the Daimler toward the compact hangar at the far end of the airport's sole runway. There appeared no one about as he brought the car to a screeching halt. He quickly found a side door and discovered it was unlocked. He pushed himself inside. Several armed guards surrounded a large group of children, perhaps thirty or forty in number. They were huddled there on the concrete floor, many of them crying, some of them horrendously young. One of the guards noted Max's presence and raised his rifle.

"You're in the wrong place, buddy," the guard said.

Some of the children screamed; their sobbing intensified. They were all obviously deathly afraid of what would happen next.

"Those who prey upon children, the most innocent," a familiar voice boomed, "will face the harshest of judgments."

Seemingly out of nowhere, The Wraith appeared. The guard who had spoken fired but missed his target. Others rushed at the Dread Avenger all at once. Despite The Wraith's recent ordeal, Max was stunned to see The Wraith in full flight, taking care of each armed guard with mighty blow after mighty blow.

The first guard fired again. This time The Wraith wrapped himself in his bullet-proof cloak. The instant the barrage ended, he spread his cape out and wide, and launched himself at the armed thug. The Wraith's anger was ferocious, and he gave the thug a beating he wouldn't soon forget.

Max was finally able to take a breath and began to move over to console as best he could. The pitiable children. He felt a harsh prod to the back of his head.

"Not today, wise guy."

Max turned slowly to find an automatic pistol shoved into his face. The man holding the weapon was, judging by Lady Wraith's description, Agent Gibbs.

"Those kids are too valuable to let free," Gibbs said.

Max saw The Wraith make a beeline for him, but Gibbs grabbed Max, held a tight arm around his throat, and lifted the gun to Max's temple.

"Don't be a hero, tough guy," Gibbs said, "or your friend's brains get aerated."

The Wraith stopped cold, watching Gibbs intently. Max knew he was assessing the situation, measuring his options, waiting for the moment to strike. Max also knew despite the circumstances appearing grim, he was in safe hands.

"Leave now and maybe–*maybe*–I let this guy live," Gibbs said. "Those kids are going nowhere."

"These innocents are under my protection," The Wraith boomed. "I will not let you harm them."

"Hey," Gibbs said in a cheery, smarmy fashion, "I'm not gonna harm a hair on their heads. That's for others, not me."

"You bastard," Max whispered through gritted teeth.

"Hey, hey," Gibbs said, tightening his grip around Max's throat, "be nice. Your life is at stake here."

"I would" –Max spat in anger– "gladly give my life for these children."

"Tough words," Gibbs said with a mocking tone. "You just might get your wish."

The Wraith scowled, gnashed his teeth. Max knew it was all about to blow up in Gibbs' face. Max felt Gibbs' grip relax ever-so-slightly. No doubt the arrogant agent thought he was in such a commanding position he thought he could loosen up, if only slightly, but Max knew this was the opportunity they had been waiting for. He quickly thrust his left elbow back, slammed it into Gibb's stomach, causing the agent to let him go. Max dived sideways, out of the way of what was to come.

Max barely caught sight of the action that followed. The Wraith grabbed his grapnel gun from his belt and fired it directly at Gibbs. The agent didn't know what hit him, the grappling hook smashed into Gibbs' shoulder, drawing both screams of agony and blood. Gibbs fired his weapon wildly. The Wraith, clearly in no mood for talk, yanked harshly at the grapnel line, which sent Gibbs pummeling toward him. When Gibbs reached The Wraith, the Dread Avenger lashed out with as powerful a blow as Max had ever witnessed. He could almost swear he felt the vibrations of the punch through the hangar floor. Gibbs flew backward through the air at high speed, crashing into the nearest wall, causing shards of brick and debris to spew out. Max thought he heard bones crack. Gibbs landed in a heap on the floor, out for the count, badly wounded.

Max scrambled to his feet in time to see The Wraith crumple to his knees. "Chief!" he cried. Such an exhibition of power had clearly taken it out of him.

"I'm...okay," The Wraith rasped. "Just a little weak. Give me a moment to catch my breath." The Wraith looked over at the children, all seated nearby, crying and whimpering in abject terror. "Max...I have a small bus parked nearby, *borrowed* from the local school. Help me up."

Max did so. The Wraith stood and stretched his body, quickly appearing as he always did. Even after all he had been through, his strength and vitality amazed the Irishman. The Wraith made his way slowly toward the children.

"My friend and I are here to help you," The Wraith said softly and gently. "We are here to take you to safety."

A small girl, perhaps no more than five or six years of age, tears in her eyes, bravely stood and took a few steps toward The Wraith. "I want my mommy."

The Wraith crouched down. Max could see his eyes were glistening with tears as well. "Sweetie...I'll find your mommy, I promise. You'll all return to your homes now."

The little girl paused for a moment then launched herself at The Wraith, wrapping her arms around him in a tear-filled hug. The Wraith took her in his arms and embraced her warmly.

"It'll be okay," he whispered. "Everything will be okay now. Nobody will ever hurt you."

Max watched on, smiling, for what felt like an eternity. Only after the two partially separated did he realize he too was weeping. These poor children.

With the little girl still in The Wraith's arms, the other children, emboldened by this, had moved over and joined her, surrounding them all.

"What's your name?" The Wraith asked the little girl.

"Emily," she replied. "Emily Roseanne."

The Wraith smiled, stood, and picked Emily up. She wrapped her arms around his neck. "Emily Roseanne...let's go home."

The children cheered as The Wraith, Emily, and Max led them out the rear entrance. Max felt some trepidation. Lady Wraith was still back there, but he realized the children would always be their top priority. He knew The Wraith would feel the same way.

# ~ Chapter 14 ~

"**W**hat the hell do you think you're doing?"

"You have the right to remain silent," Sloan started.

"To hell with you," the man spat. "Don't you know who I am?"

"I know full well, sir," Sloan said, "but the law applies to everyone equally, even those in City Hall."

"You sonuva..." The deputy mayor stopped short, perhaps thinking better of the situation. "You're finished in the force, you hear me?"

Commissioner Harrison stepped forth from amongst the growing throng of police officers milling about in the front yard of Deputy Mayor Sargent's home. "Mr. Deputy Mayor, sir, you are being arrested on suspicion of being involved in a child sex ring. If you would allow my officers to read you your rights, we can proceed to headquarters."

"What are you talking about?" Sargent said, outraged as his wife joined him at the front door.

"Jim, what's this all about?" she said, clearly confused and a little apprehensive. She placed a hand on her husband's shoulder.

"Nothing, dear, this is just some sort of...misunderstanding," Sargent said, evidently becoming more nervous.

"We have evidence," Sloan said, dispensing with the "sir." Such platitudes, especially under the circumstances, galled him. "Enough to put you away for a *very* long time. Now, let me do my job and we can get this over with."

Sargent's bluster and fury evaporated at the word *evidence*. He turned to face his wife, tried to smile but nothing really came. He moved to pat her hand, but she withdrew it when she realized the truth. Her face darkened. So did his. His whole body sagged as he allowed his Miranda rights to be read, then was carted off by two officers.

Sloan turned to Harrison as they walked to their respective cars parked in the street. "That's a dozen already. With more to come."

"Some big fry, still. We'll bring them all in by the book. Then it's all up to the D.A. We'll have done our bit," Harrison said.

Sloan took a deep breath. It had been a long night, and there was still plenty to come. The deputy mayor was just the latest to be arrested. They had already taken in lawyers, a well-known TV newscaster, a few business executives, and a popular radio personality. All had been featured on the list supplied by Lady Wraith. All the repulsive details of their connection to the sex ring were clear and conclusive. Sloan only hoped they all would never see the light of day again. That freedom would forever be denied them. Then, and only then, would he feel as though a small modicum of justice had been served.

"Let's get to it then, sir," Sloan finally said to the commissioner.

\* \* \* \* \* \* \*

Lady Wraith tensed her muscles in preparation for the battle ahead. Her mind was still awhirl at the sight before her-Blackstorm alive. She had seen him die at his own hand, confirmed that herself. How it was now possible she was facing him again, she could not fathom.

Blackstorm emitted a deep, guttural laugh. "You are confused, I can see. Perhaps you have met another of my brethren. He was but one of many that serve our master. We are all Blackstorm to him."

Now Lady Wraith understood. At least she could console herself she was not going mad. Small consolation, though. This Blackstorm was no doubt fresh and battle-ready. Trepidation coursed through Lady Wraith's veins. She had bested the previous Blackstorm, that much was true, but that almost felt like a lifetime ago, and it took everything she had to do so. And she still felt the pain of that mêlée. Was she truly ready to do it all again? She would soon see. She had no other choice.

"I defeated the last Blackstorm that crossed my path," Lady Wraith said, trying to provoke her enemy with a show of bravado. "I will deal with you the same way."

"Then let us tarry no longer."

Blackstorm advanced, obviously choosing to go on the offensive rather than wait. He was startlingly fast, despite his large size. He lashed out with powerful blows, which Lady Wraith only just managed to avoid. She tried to take a few backward steps to get some room, get her bearings, but Blackstorm was too fast. He reached out and took her in his arms in a mighty bear hug. He lifted her off the ground and squeezed tightly.

"Ugh," Lady Wraith gasped, her breath crushed out of her.

"You are nothing," Blackstorm said. "Nothing but a weak, insipid female. I will flatten you like the bug you are."

He tightened his grip. Lady Wraith was sure she felt a rib snap, pain engulfing her torso. She could barely breathe and started seeing spots before her very eyes.

*No, not now, not like this.*

Her arms were pinned to her side. No amount of struggle could move them, let alone free them. She was now totally in Blackstorm's thrall. But wait...could she reach her belt with her hands, her right hand in particular? She wiggled and squirmed. Yes, maybe...just about there. The button...done. The Eyes on her chest burst to life.

"Arrggh!" Blackstorm screamed as he reached up to his eyes and staggered backwards, dropping Lady Wraith in the process.

Lady Wraith sagged to her knees in agony and desperately tried to fill her lungs with air. It hurt to breathe, but she knew she had to press forward her advantage. Blackstorm wasn't truly blinded, not without further exposure to her Eyes of Judgment, and she preferred not to resort to that unless forced to. Or, worse, use her disintegrating Judgment Stare.

She lurched to her feet and took a few tentative steps toward her adversary. Blackstorm still flailed about blind, rubbing at his eyes, clearly disoriented and struggling. It was now or never. With an exuberant cry, she lashed out with a right, then a left, followed by another one-two. Blackstorm, unable to see the hits coming, could do nothing to avoid them. His head flung backward, left and right with each successive strike to his face. Lady Wraith followed that with vicious knees to Blackstorm's stomach. Even with his body armor, he obviously felt the attack and curled over in pain.

Adrenalin, and the rush of success, began to overwhelm Lady Wraith. She was doing it again, succeeding in overpowering an enemy as powerful and as accomplished as Blackstorm. She couldn't help but smile. She would end it now.

Suddenly, with a guttural rasp, Blackstorm was up and crash-tackled Lady Wraith, the two pummeling down onto the asphalt. They rolled around, wrestling, struggling for their lives. Blackstorm lashed out with several punches to Lady Wraith's face. Blood was spilled. She spat it into Blackstorm's face, then slammed a fist into his face in return. Blackstorm rotated his body, positioning himself on top of Lady Wraith, trying to use his body weight to gain the upper hand. She kneed him in the jaw, shattering some teeth in the process, and wormed herself free.

She scrambled to her feet, preparing for the battle to continue. Blackstorm did likewise. She pressed at a button on her belt's right side and her Eyes of Judgment burst into bright life once again. She hoped not to use them, wished that Blackstorm would think better of continuing their clash. Upon spying the Eyes of Judgment, Blackstorm relaxed his limbs a little...and turned and ran.

Caught off-guard somewhat by this turn of events, Lady Wraith took a few seconds to react, then sprinted after her opponent. Though every step brought forward a stabbing pain in her chest, she ignored it as best she could. She wasn't about to let Blackstorm escape. The villain had just entered the plane through the lengthy rear ramp when Lady Wraith reached him. She grabbed him by the shoulder and spun him around. He retaliated with a backward slap, sending Lady Wraith careening back down the ramp. Before she could really come to her senses, the airplane roared to life and the ramp began to lift. The plane started to taxi down the runway.

*Oh no you don't.*

Despite the pain, in spite of the fatigue, Lady Wraith leapt to her feet and sprinted in pursuit. The plane, its ramp now closed, was starting to slowly build up speed. She couldn't let Blackstorm get away. She ran faster than she had ever done before and finally began to gain some ground on the craft. Her lungs burning, her body aching, but with maximum effort, she managed to reach the plane. But now what?

There was a small handhold beside the left side door, and without further thought, she grabbed for it. As she did, the plane began to lift into the air and, within seconds, was airborne–with Lady Wraith clutching for her life to the plane's side.

She held on firmly, but the wind and pressure being exerted upon her body was becoming harder and harder to withstand. Her cape billowed around her. The plane continued its upward trajectory, bound for who knew where. Lady Wraith knew she had to act quickly. Once they'd reach a certain height, she would struggle for air and freeze, if she were able to hold on that long. Remaining outside was not an option. A small charge to blow the side door open was her only viable alternative, but to do that, she had to reach down to her belt to retrieve it, which meant hanging on by only one hand. She had to do it, the only other choice to let go, glide safely back to the ground, but allow Blackstorm to escape. She wasn't willing to do that. Her resolve was firm. She would risk it all to take Blackstorm down.

She reached down to her belt with her left hand, remaining attached to the plane with her stronger right hand. Even so, within those few seconds, she almost lost her grip twice. It took everything she had to stay in position. She quickly placed the charge in position and hunched under her cape as some small measure of protection from the blast. A further few seconds and an explosion tore the door clean off its hinges, flinging outward past Lady Wraith out into the air. How she managed to hold on, Heaven only knew, but she didn't delay any further, twisting her body and swinging inside the relative safety of the plane.

Once inside, she took a moment to catch her breath, but only a moment. She somehow had to constrain Blackstorm and then bring the plane back around and land it at the airport safely. All this was assuming there was nobody else on board she had to deal with as well. She hoped that to be the case. Either way, she had a job to do. She wasn't about to let herself fail now.

She found herself in the rear cargo area of the plane, no doubt where the children were to have been placed. It was devoid of any furniture or hardware, appearing completely stripped down. Thankfully, as she had thought, there was nobody about. She hoped that would remain so once she reached the cockpit. Unfortunately, the blast she had caused to gain entry had undoubtedly forewarned Blackstorm–or anyone else–of her likely presence, so a surprise attack may no longer be an option.

As she briefly mulled over her potential plans, a door at the far end of the cargo bay before her tore open, revealing Blackstorm in all his furious glory.

"My eyes still burn," Blackstorm growled, "but I see." He stepped forth into the cargo bay. "You have pursued me to your grave. Let us end this now!"

Without another word, he charged her with astonishing speed, slamming into her and sending them both smashing into the wall. Lady Wraith slumped there, the wind knocked from her, but she rallied swiftly. Taking her enemy a little by surprise, she retaliated with an attack of her own. Before he could prepare a defense, she lashed out with quickfire punches to his face and body. She knew it was now or never. Don't let up, keep up the assault, let fly with all she had. With a cry, she laced into him, not wavering for even a moment. Punch after punch, kick after kick, knee after knee. No matter how tired or in pain she was, she did not waver. Not with so much at stake.

At last, after a barrage any lesser man would have crumbled under, Blackstorm fell. Lady Wraith, utterly exhausted, almost joined him in a heap on the cargo bay floor, but she managed to collect herself. Just.

Tired beyond belief, and with every joint aching, Lady Wraith stretched her back, trying to straighten and regain her composure. The plane. She had to take control of the plane. She turned, saw the still-open door and made her way through it, out through a narrow gangway and ultimately into the cockpit. As she had expected, the plane was operating on autopilot. The compass indicated they were traveling in a northerly direction.

*North? Boston? Montreal?*

It mattered not. This plane was heading back to Metro City pronto and Blackstorm would be held to account for his heinous actions. She took the controls and geared the plane around, back toward home.

"Ack!"

Lady Wraith was met with a searing pain in her head and a ringing in her ears. Unconsciousness beckoned, but she held it together long enough to turn and see Blackstorm, wielding what appeared to be a tire iron, ready to strike her again. If he did so, she would be done for. This was it. She reached to her belt, activated her Eyes of Judgment.

"Let all who are guilty face the ultimate judgment," she cried. The blinding Judgment Stare caught Blackstorm full in the face and he was unable to avoid it. He yelped in pain and, perhaps, panic, dropping the tire iron and reaching up to his eyes.

"You've blinded me!" he shouted. He ripped his mask from his head to reveal a non-descript male of maybe late twenties in age, with short brown hair, clean shaven. He could have been anyone. He could have been the guy next door. "You'll pay for this!"

He pulled a lengthy dagger from his belt and proceeded to madly swipe here and there. Even blinded as he was, the cockpit was cramped, and Lady Wraith knew he would likely connect at some point unless she retreated to a more open space. Blackstorm raised the weapon above his head, intending to plunge it deep within his opponent, but Lady Wraith managed to twist her body to one side, avoiding the death blow. The dagger embedded instead into the plane's control panel, causing sparks to fly and warning signals to blare.

*Oh no! The controls are jammed. There's no way I'll be able to pilot and land this safely.*

Blackstorm, mad with vengeance, didn't appear to care. He readied to attack again. Quickly, Lady Wraith sent a powerful kick into Blackstorm's groin, causing him to groan and double over. She followed that up with a knee to the face, flattening Blackstorm's nasal septum, blood splattering everywhere.

With Blackstorm momentarily incapacitated, Lady Wraith took one last look through the plane's windshield. The airport's runway was visible in the distance. The plane was progressing on a downward trajectory. There was no way of controlling or stopping it. She had to grab Blackstorm and make their escape from the rear of the plane before it was too late.

Lady Wraith yanked her enemy to his feet. The fight had gone out of him.

"Let's go, we haven't moments to lose," she said.

Blackstorm looked at her briefly through what Lady Wraith thought were saddened eyes. Had he perhaps thought better of the entire venture? Was he somehow feeling a sense of remorse? The moment instantly passed, and Lady Wraith heard a cracking sound...and Blackstorm sagged to the floor, dead. Probably a cyanide capsule.

*Have it your way.*

She bolted for the rear side door with which she had entered the craft. She peered out, saw the airport looming...and leaped. Using her cape to somewhat slow her descent, Lady Wraith nevertheless crashed into the tarmac, somehow managing to contort her body in a roll, and spun round and round until, finally, she came to a halt.

Battered, bruised, but alive.

She had only seconds to raise her head and see the plane crash into the small hangar at the far end of the runway, the structure erupting into a massive ball of flame that both shot upward and outward all at once. Even from her safe distance, she felt the intensity of the blast and heat from the conflagration. It was at this moment she remembered the children. She was overwhelmed with a feeling of dread and sadness. She could only hope Max had managed to get them–and anyone else that might have been in there–to safety in time.

Lady Wraith was spent. She had never known such weariness, such pain, such...anything. Her mind was a muddle of thoughts, emotions, and questions. It hurt to think. She needed a rest. Even though she was out in the open as she was, she lay herself down. She needed to breathe, to hope...

And to pray.

# ~ Epilogue ~

**S**ooki opened the door to find Robert Anderson, still bandaged up but appearing in something of a good mood, standing in her threshold. She embraced him.

"Hey, hey," Anderson said with a smile on his face, "I'm still injured here."

"Of course, I'm sorry," Sooki said, somewhat chagrined.

Anderson stroked her cheek gently. "It's okay, I was joking."

She smiled weakly at him and allowed him to enter her compact apartment. "You must be feeling better if you've come to visit me. Clearly you're not too damaged...down there."

Anderson frowned at her. "That's not what I'm here for."

"Really," Sooki said with some surprise. "That's a first."

"Don't be like that," Anderson said. "I'm trying to say something, I'm trying to..."

He stopped short. Sooki could see he was struggling. Had she been too hard on him? Life had been tough, was still tough, on her, but Anderson had been the only one who had shown her any sort of kindness, the only one who had appeared to care. She cared, too, but...it was difficult.

"It's okay, I'm sorry. Bad day. Bad week. Bad month. Bad life." Life truly was beginning to wear her down.

Anderson stroked her hair. Sooki now noticed he was gentler, softer somehow, less stressed. She liked it.

"This latest case has...taught me something, Sooki," Anderson said. "Life is too short. Life is precious. I've neglected mine for too long now." He paced about. "Work has been my life. I've never been good with women, with feelings, with anything but work. So, I let it take over my life, let it become my life. Let my ambition be the only thing keeping me going. Until I met you."

Sooki couldn't believe what she was hearing. She was nothing, just a cheap hooker, a former runaway and junkie. And now this? What the heck. She didn't deserve this, none of this.

"I...I..." But nothing else came to her.

"I know, I should have said all this sooner. I'm not...good at this sort of thing."

"What *are* you trying to say, Robert?" Sooki said softly, moving in close to him.

"Look...I cashed out my retirement, handed in my notice with the force. I'm done with all this. I'm moving away. I've had enough with Metro City. I'll find something else to do."

Sooki's heart sank for a moment. Perhaps it had been all too good to be true after all. "Oh."

"And I want you to come with me," Anderson said, gripping Sooki gently by the shoulders. "We can start a new life together. I have enough to set us up. We can both find something else to do."

Sooki's eyes welled with tears. It's exactly what she'd always wanted to hear but never truly thought she would. She didn't think she was worth such words. "You...really mean it, Robert?"

He took her in his arms and gave her a kiss. "I mean it. Let's leave this hellhole behind us. We can find better out there. Be better people...together."

They embraced again, tears streaming down Sooki's cheeks. She had never known such joy. Sometimes good things happened to those, perhaps, less worthy.

Or maybe she was worth something after all.

\* \* \* \* \* \* \*

Sloan was just logging off his computer in the early hours of the morning, preparing to head home and hit the sheets. He was done in. A full night of arrests and interviews. He felt exhilaration at the knowledge they had broken the sex ring wide open and brought many of the perpetrators to justice, but was downcast knowing the ringleader–or leaders–had gotten away with it. Not even their identities were known. That galled him to no end. Harrison had told him to take solace with the knowledge many children had been saved, and many people would be spending the rest of their lives in prison. Sloan knew all this full well, but in some ways, it was small comfort. The big fry had escaped, and that was something Sloan felt was hard to live with.

"Penny for your thoughts," a familiar voice said.

Sloan turned to see his partner, Rosa Perez, standing opposite him in front of her own desk. She was smiling and appeared happier and healthier than she had in quite some time. He was overjoyed to see her.

"Perez," Sloan said, "you're back."

"Back and raring to go," she said with a smile.

"Man, we could have used you on this case," Sloan said. "It was a tough one."

Perez rounded the desk and approached her partner, placing a consoling hand on his shoulder. "I'm sorry I wasn't there for you."

Sloan suddenly felt bad. He hadn't meant it that way, hadn't meant to make Perez feel guilty for looking after herself. "No, I'm sorry. I know you took some time off to get away, sort yourself out. I didn't mean to..."

"I know, Bob. I know," Perez said. "Lola at the front desk filled me in on the case. I can't believe how far-reaching the conspiracy went. Even the FBI."

Sloan nodded grimly. "Some in the precinct here, some in other precincts in the city. Others in every echelon of society. We just spent the night corralling them all. APB put out on those identified outside the city, throughout the country."

Perez whistled. It was the largest such bust in US history.

Sloan rubbed the back of his neck. "Well, enough of that...how are you? Did you...sort through things?"

Perez smiled, appeared relaxed and comfortable in her own skin. "I'm feeling much better, thank you. Got out of the city, into some fresh air. Relaxed. A bit of sunshine. Just the right tonic."

"And that...feeling...?"

"Is gone. And if it comes back...I'll know what to do," Perez said with a smile.

Sloan matched her smile with one of his own, immediately followed by a long, deep yawn.

"Go home. Get some rest," Perez said.

"I had intended to. Job's done for the day...and night. Now it's up to the D.A. and his team."

"Until tomorrow," Perez said.

"Until tomorrow, when we do it all again."

"I'll be here."

Sloan stood, took his jacket from the back of his chair. Perez gave him a quick, warm hug. "Good to have you back, partner."

Perez smiled again then went back to her desk, picked up some paperwork, and began to read. Sloan watched her briefly before heading toward the stairwell that led to the station's front desk and then to the exit.

\* \* \* \* \* \* \*

It was weeks later, and Paul and Leena were seated in the library, about to take their morning coffee.

"Ahh...that coffee smells divine," Leena said.

"Vittoria Espresso," Paul said with a twinkle in his eye as he poured them both a cup from the silver coffee pot. "Your favorite."

"I don't think I could get through a morning without a cup," Leena said, taking a sip from her fine bone china cup.

"Nor I," Paul said.

Leena placed her cup on the small table in front of her and eyed Paul carefully. Since their ordeal, he had healed– certainly physically–but mentally? Leena wasn't so sure. Paul had yet to fully talk of his experience. At least he was now wearing his new Marinor dive watch.

"So...are we going to talk about what we all went through? What *you* went through?" Leena said finally.

Paul sighed, whether through difficulty or resignation, Leena couldn't tell. He took another sip from his cup. "I'm sorry we haven't discussed things yet. It's not due to any injury, physical or mental, on my part. Apart from initially being beaten, then shackled, I was not tortured or abused in any way, but...knowing what those children were about to go through, what others *have* been through, continue to go through...it churns my stomach. It's not something I enjoy bringing back to mind."

"I know how you feel," was all Leena could manage to say, then added, "but we did manage to destroy that ring and save many of the children before any true harm had come to them."

"Physical harm, at least," Paul added. "Mental...well, let's hope in time all will be well."

"They'll heal. They're back with their loving families. With love and some professional care, I'm sure they'll fully recover."

"Mmm..." Paul said. His face clouded over with concern.

"Paul? What is it?"

"Your mention of loving families," he said. "It's true, we were able to reunite all the children with their families...save one."

Leena was surprised to hear this.

"Emily Roseanne. Her mother...committed suicide after Emily had been taken, when it became apparent she wasn't likely to come home." Paul's demeanor was downcast.

"Oh no."

"Emily has no other family. None. She's all on her own," Paul said, tears coming to his eyes.

"What will happen to her?" Leena said.

"Foster care. She'll likely be shuttled from household to household. That's often the way within the system."

"Awful," Leena said after a few moments' thought.

"Leena?"

"Yes?"

"I have a suggestion. It's a big change, will be a big change to our lives, but...I thought we'd become pretty used to that over the years," Paul said. "Emily Roseanne...she's a beautiful little girl. We have the money, the space...I know our lives are not exactly routine, but with a little adjustment, I know we could–"

"Wait...what? What are you asking of me?" Leena said.

"Maybe we could adopt her?" Paul said. "Like I said, it's a big change to our lives, but if you'd seen her little face, held her as I did...I couldn't bear to abandon her to the system. We'll be married soon, and we have all the love she could ever need."

"But The Wraith, the life we live..."

"We could make this work, I know we could," Paul said.

Leena thought it over. A child in their lives, so soon and one already nearing school age, with the lives they lead...it was a lot to take in right there and then. But, as she thought about it, it started to make sense. The love was there. That's all that mattered. This little girl needed them. Needed love.

"Let's do it," Leena said at last. "This little girl needs us."

Paul smiled, his mood definitely lifting.

"I just wish..." Leena said after a minute.

"What, honey?"

"As well as this case ultimately turned out, as successful as we had been...I just wish we had been able to at least identify who was the person or persons at the very top. Even without any direct evidence, with their identity known, we could further target them..."

"I know exactly who they are, who the Head is, or should I say, was," Paul said.

"What?" Leena said, completely stunned. "How?"

"You forget, I was in the belly of the beast. No doubt they thought I wouldn't survive the experience so freely talked around me. The Head of the ring was our dearly departed enemy, Robert Latham."

Leena couldn't help but gasp at this revelation. She well knew how evil Latham was, knew he was the spider in the center of Metro's web of deceit...but this? She somehow thought Latham was beyond such depredation.

"I can see your surprise," Paul said.

"I don't know why I am, but..."

"Whether Latham knew of his deputy's...predilections...or not, who can say," Paul continued. "As far as I can tell, this was just another way for Latham to make money and to exert power. With so many of the high and mighty in society partaking in this wickedness, it was easy for Latham to both protect and control them in a way he couldn't with his other business enterprises. For him, that's what it's always been about–money and power."

"But what of the new head of Latham Industries?" Leena said.

"Patrich Azufi?" Paul said. "That fool? Oh, he knows all about the sex ring, naturally, but he has no interest in it. His interest was in me, in auctioning off my identity to the highest bidder."

"Which reminds me," Leena said. "Blackstorm...they had a cobra emblazoned on their chest. They kept talking about their master..."

"Yes, I know," Paul said. "I don't have any answers to your obvious questions, but...I'm going to find out."

Leena feared the worst. The Cobra...alive? It didn't seem possible, yet a body had never been found. Was he alive? Had he returned after all this time? It was a terrible thought, but at least it was one for another day.

"It's starting on the television now, sir," Simpson said, poking his head into the room.

"Hmm? Oh, thank you, Simpson," Paul said.

"Something on TV?" Leena said.

Paul nodded and reached for the remote on the table beside the coffee service. He flicked the switch and the large flatscreen television burst to life. "An announcement from Latham Industries."

Leena was perplexed. Even when Latham was alive it wasn't like him to appear on TV like this. Interviews, yes, press conferences, occasionally, but public announcements? Unheard of. "What could this be about?"

"I doubt it's anything too important. Latham Industries is probably just announcing a new CEO to replace that fop Patrich Azufi. Or perhaps they're going under."

"Surely not," Leena replied to the last portion of his statement.

Paul moved over and sat next to Leena, waiting for the announcement to commence.

"There, it's starting at last," Leena said.

Leena took another sip of her coffee and ruminated on the recent past. Over the past few months, Metro City had been largely devastated by the villain Crossfire, whose mad schemes of revenge saw the loss of countless lives, most notably those of crime lord Robert Latham, his erstwhile lackey Charlie Grieco, and Latham's possibly short-lived successor, Patrich Azufi did not get off scot free either. More recently, Paul had been kidnapped, and the entire city embroiled in a nationwide conspiracy. It was almost too much to think about. And now, on this fine morning, something concerning Latham Industries. Leena would have rather been out and about on such a lovely, sunny day.

"Mayor Hutchison is about to speak," Paul said with a hint of surprise. "What does he have to do with Latham Industries?"

Leena looked on with intense interest.

"Ladies and gentlemen," Hutchison said into the camera in a stern voice, shifting his short, rubicund body somewhat uncomfortably, "as you know, this city has seen its fair share of tragedy in recent months. Gang violence, terrorist attacks. And, just last night, our city's finest conducted the largest arrest of its kind in this country's history. Prior to that, many innocent lives were lost, most notably my good friend and this city's patron, Robert Latham."

Paul snorted at that.

"Since his death, and the...incapacitation of his successor, Patrich Azufi..." Hutchison continued.

*Incapacitation?* Leena thought. *Since when?*

"...the company has naturally suffered. Its stock price has plummeted, offices have shuttered, jobs have been lost. And this city's fortunes have waned along with that of this fine company."

"He's laying it on thick," Paul said, rolling his eyes. "Even if the company is folding, it's hardly worthy of such a grandiose public declaration."

"However," Hutchison continued, his face brightening slightly, "amid all the doom and gloom, I can hereby announce there is hope. Hope for Metro City. Latham Industries is on the precipice of a new age of success and prosperity. Its destiny is to carry this great city forward along with it as it always has in the past."

"Oh please," Paul blurted, rolling his eyes once again. Leena's thoughts mirrored Paul's.

"Only one person can guarantee such an outcome. Now..." Hutchison continued with his narrative, pausing briefly for effect, smiling the entire time, "...this will no doubt come as a great shock to you all. It did to me only yesterday. But it has also brought me great joy...which I know you will all share with me. I am so very pleased to announce the CEO of Latham Industries, the man who is ready, willing and able to rescue the company, and the city as a whole—"

Paul sat bolt upright, his eyes bulging. Leena turned from the TV to Paul and back again.

"—is actually its original CEO; its founder, and this city's great patron, Mr. Robert Latham!"

Leena couldn't believe what she was seeing or hearing. She felt numb—and knew Paul would feel likewise—as though she was suffering from shock. She turned to Paul, whose jaw had almost crashed down to the floor. He returned her gaze, then both returned their vision to the TV. There, on the screen in front of them, hobbling into camera, was indeed Robert Latham, their great nemesis. The man appeared older, somehow, and he needed a cane to walk, but the expression on his face—in his eyes—confirmed his identity at once.

He was alive.

# ~ Author's Note ~

This story has long been in my mind. It was originally intended as something of a spin off of the main series, but then I thought...why not include it as a volume in the series after all? It was an important enough story, a female superhero taking charge in her own, full blown adventure, but then I thought to make the stakes even higher–The Wraith is missing and only Lady Wraith can find her? My co-author, Adam Oravec, came up with the hard hitting plotline featuring child trafficking, and then the story really came into its own. Lady Wraith would tackle not some mystical creature, not some superpowered adversary, but the most heinous of real life crimes of all.

I'd like to thank my co-author, for really inspiring me with his original plot, and to my family, who are always there for me when I need them. I hope my daughter, Emma, when she grows older, will enjoy this story of female empowerment.

I hope all my readers enjoy this story as well. It's an old fashioned pulp story a little more in the style of Chandler or MacDonald, but featuring a costumed superhero. I'm proud of it.

Keep an eye for a preview of the next novel in the series, *Kingdom*, in the coming pages. It'll be out roughly around mid-2025. You won't want to miss it.

Take care
Frank Dirscherl
Wollongong, 2025

## ~ Sneak peek ~

Here is a special sneak peek at the following novel in the series, *Kingdom*. Please enjoy chapter 1 of this exciting book...

# ~ Chapter 1 ~

Paul could feel the sweat pouring down his brow. His throat was suddenly parched in a way he hadn't experienced since his predecessor's time in the Eritrean desert. It was as though he couldn't move, frozen in time in this spot.

*Is that a voice I hear?*

"Darling? Paul! Snap out of it!"

That did it. Paul looked into her beautiful eyes and came back to himself. He returned his attention to the television screen.

"Mr Latham will now explain his miraculous return himself," Hutchison concluded by way of introduction.

"Thank you, John," Latham said, his voice a little weaker, yet still determined, the tone still sharp and cruel. "I stand before you a changed man. A humbled man. When that terrorist...Crossfire? —he turned to Mayor Hutchison, who nodded in somber reply— "attacked me in my home, I managed to escape into a protective bunker in the basement.

That quick-thinking saved my life, though the blast was so powerful, it nevertheless cost me my right leg." He tapped at the leg with his cane. It gave off a solid thud.

"Oh my," Leena uttered.

"But worse still, it cost me the life of my dear wife. Oh my darling." Latham bowed his head, tears welled in his eyes.

*He almost looks authentic,* Paul thought, then wondered if he was perhaps being too harsh on the man. Even Adolf Hitler loved his wife, after all.

Latham took the seat offered to him by the mayor and composed himself before continuing. "When I came to, I had no memory of who I was or how I came to have such catastrophic injuries. All I knew was that I needed help if I was to survive. I managed to crawl from the wreckage of my home, used a plank to help me walk down to the street, where I flagged down a motorist, and...and..."

The crime lord choked up, and appeared unable to continue his amazing story.

"It's all right," Hutchison said, stepping in and consoling his friend. "Ladies and gentlemen, Mr Latham's office will be releasing a full statement to the press shortly, outlining the remainder of my good friend's story. I think we had better finish—"

"No," Latham said sharply. "No," he repeated, gently this time, "allow me a few more words." He took a deep breath. "Suffice to say, when I finally came to myself, I vowed to save this city. My wife often told me she was competing for my attentions, not with another woman, but with this city. I used to laugh at that, but now...now I can perhaps see the truth in her words. I love this city. I always have. That...scum took my wife. I won't let him take my city as well."

Latham motioned to Hutchison, and the press conference came to an end, a station announcer appearing onscreen to sum up what had just occurred.

Both Paul and Leena remained silent for moments which seemingly dragged on and on.

"Well," Leena said at last. "That proved to be more than either of us had expected."

"You have a brilliant way of understating things," Paul replied with more than a hint of sarcasm.

"He's back," she whispered.

"He's back."

\* \* \* \* \* \*

"Thank you, John" Latham said, taking Hutchison's hand in his and gave it a strong shake.

"Let me know if you need anything else from me," Hutchison said.

"I'll be in touch, rest assured."

And with that, Latham crawled into the back of his waiting limousine parked in the television studio parking lot, and was soon off.

"Smithers, is it?" Latham enquired.

"Yes, sir," came the quick reply. "It's good to have you back, sir. This city will live again now that you're here."

"Yes indeed," Latham said, allowing himself the comfort of a wry smile.

*Yes, my kingdom will rise again.*

\* \* \* \* \* \*

Paul paced back and forth in the Lair, not really knowing what to think or do.

"Chief?"

"Hmm," Paul said without much thought to whom he was speaking.

"Are you okay?" Max persisted.

"Hmm," Paul repeated, before finally noticing the burly Irishman Max Horton, who had been his right hand man, his factotum, ever since he had tried to rob the original Paul Sanderson several years past in London. "Oh, Max. What is it you wanted?"

Max looked at him with some concern. "I asked if you were okay. And I don't think that you are. Is it Robert Latham?"

"As horrible as the man's murder was," Paul began while continuing to pace, "it nevertheless lifted a great weight from my shoulders. My greatest, most consistent enemy, gone. But today we find out it was little more than a dream."

A whirring of gears indicated an upstairs entry into the Lair. Leena appeared on the upper deck and, after descending in the micro-elevator, quickly joined them.

"I thought you'd be down here," she said to Paul.

"I'll tell you something," Paul said to Max, "I don't buy his coma story. Someone as well known in Metro as Robert Latham and the hospital he's in doesn't recognize him? Please. Something doesn't add up."

"You're right," Leena said, her face brightening. "There's no way we wouldn't have known of his survival before now, not if it all happened as he claims. What could he be up to?"

"Your guess is as good as mine," Paul said. "But it can't be good. And with this terrible drug epidemic in Metro at present...this is the last thing we need right now."

Leena and Max gave each other a knowing glance.

"Whatever Latham is planning...I have a feeling we won't have long to wait to find out."

\* \* \* \* \* \*

Patrich Azufi groaned as he woke. He was momentarily confused. Everything was foggy in his mind.

*Where am I? What is this?*

His head throbbed with the migraine of the century. He moved to grab at his head—but his right arm wouldn't budge. Panic gripped him, he felt his entire body shudder and the sweat began to flow.

*What's going on? Why can't I move properly?*

He looked about him. He was in a small, cramped bedroom. Very pink, very girly.

"Help!" Azufi screamed, almost involuntarily. "Help me!"

"Darling?" a sweet, feminine voice came from just outside the door. A gorgeous young lady appeared, long blonde hair, wearing a nurse's uniform. Curves in all the right places, her appearance in the open door brought it all back to Azufi. "It's all right, sweetie," Maggie-Grace Clifford, Azufi's nurse during his recent hospital stay, said, bending over and giving him a soft peck on the cheek. "Did you have another nightmare?"

"No," Azufi grunted. "I just...forgot where I was for a moment."

"Oh dear. Well, are you all right now? I really have to go to work."

"Must you?" Azufi said, almost pleading, which surprised him. "You know I hate being left alone."

"And you know I have to work," she said, "this apartment isn't cheap, and your disability check still hasn't turned up."

"Fine, fine," Azufi grumbled.

"Now, I've made you your breakfast already, just head in to the kitchen and plonk yourself down," she said with a smile. "And, we'll have some *fun* tonight when I get home. I know you'll like that."

And with that, and a blown kiss, she was gone.

Azufi struggled to sit up in bed. His right arm was lame, a consequence of the explosion he and Maggie-Grace had been caught up in while heading for her car in the hospital parking lot. The fact that he had convinced her to sneak him out of the hospital, with the intention of having sex at her place, is what saved his life that day. His voracious appetite was, in that case, his savior. The irony was not lost on him.

Nevertheless, the blast had caused him grievous injuries, damage to his spinal cord which left him partially paralyzed down his right side. He had tried continuing to work at Latham Industries, but he had found it extremely difficult to function at his best, then suddenly received word that he'd been fired, the board having chosen another man, thus far unknown to him, to replace him.

The reality of his situation hit him once again—he was an invalid, disabled, good for nothing—being cared for, propped up, by a bimbo hick with no money and no future, living in a minuscule dump of an apartment. But damn was she good in bed.

He tried to stand, but his muscles ached and trembled in protest. He reached for his stick with his left hand, but fumbled with it, causing it to crash to the floor.

"Damn it!" Azufi cried out. "And damn you, Crossfire, for doing this to me. To *me*!"

He plopped down on the bed and gripped the bridge of his nose.

*Damn it! I don't deserve this. I was a prince in this city once. Just moments ago. And now...now...*

Now he had nothing. No wife, no home, no money. Fired from Latham Industries only a few days ago, the company was stalling over his compensation payout, so he was stuck here, with the bimbo in her hellhole.

It was then he realized just how attached he'd become to Maggie-Grace. Whether it was by necessity or true affection, he knew not. Regardless, he needed her. Truly needed her.

And damn was she good in bed.

# ~ Also Available ~

**THE WRAITH**

## The Wraith Dread Avenger of the Underworld #1
# THE WRAITH
### Frank Dirscherl

In a world not far removed from our own, a city lies ravaged.
Crime overruns its streets, its citizens are helpless. Crime lord
Robert Latham holds the city in his sway. One man, however,
stands above the rest, willing to fight for freedom. That man is
The Wraith!

## NOW AVAILABLE!

### www.glowingeyesmedia.com

The Wraith Dread Avenger of the Underworld #2
# VALLEY OF EVIL
Frank Dirscherl

After the horror the Cobra unleashed upon Metro City, Paul Sanderson has recuperated, regained his strength and focus, and the city has been rebuilt while its citizens have slowly started to regroup and move forward. Into this relative calm marches Ma Tzi, the Hong Kong drug lord, who senses a weakness in resident crime lord Robert Latham's hold on the city and intends to exploit that in any way necessary. And at any cost.

## NOW AVAILABLE!

## www.glowingeyesmedia.com

CULT OF THE DAMNED

The Wraith Dread Avenger of the Underworld #4
# CULT OF THE DAMNED
Frank Dirscherl

With the city back firmly in his grasp, crime lord and entrepreneur Robert Latham is celebrating by bankrolling Metro City's 200th anniversary gala year, which includes the unveiling of a never-before-seen ancient Aztec stone carving—the Cortes Stone—at the City Gallery, a carving that has thrilled the scientific and artistic communities, but infuriated the monstrous Aztekoth.

## NOW AVAILABLE!

www.glowingeyesmedia.com

The Wraith Dread Avenger of the Underworld #5
# CRY OF THE WEREWOLF
Frank Dirscherl

Having gone through ordeal after ordeal, Paul Sanderson (aka The Wraith Dread Avenger of the Underworld ®) and his love Leena Patterson, decide to take a long overdue vacation. However, their idyll is soon shattered by an attack by a creature nobody thought could possibly exist—a werewolf. Soon, an evil so heinous makes himself known, and only The Wraith could possibly defeat it.

## NOW AVAILABLE!

### www.glowingeyesmedia.com

The Wraith Dread Avenger of the Underworld #6

# SWAMP WITCH OF SATAN'S FOREST

Frank Dirscherl & Ray MacKay

After the explosive conclusion of Cry of the Wereworlf, Paul
Sanderson (aka The Wraith) and his love, Leena Patterson, are
immediately drawn into danger again as Paul begins falling under
a deadly spell. While investigating this phenomenon, The Wraith
and Leena are unwittingly drawn into the forest–and the web–of
the alluring Swamp Witch.

## NOW AVAILABLE!

www.glowingeyesmedia.com

# The Wraith Dread Avenger of the Underworld #9
## KINGDOM
Frank Dirscherl

Crime lord Robert Latham has returned, seemingly from the dead, ready to reclaim his kingdom. Ready to take whatever steps are necessary to restock and rebuild, to recover his rightful position of power within Metro City, and he doesn't care who gets in his way. Not the authorities, not the people of his beloved city...and certainly not The Wraith Dread Avenger of the Underworld.

## COMING SOON!

www.glowingeyesmedia.com

## The Wraith Dread Avenger of the Underworld
### #10
# CITY OF FEAR
#### Frank Dirscherl

The Wraith's arch-nemesis, the Cobra, has returned after years being presumed dead. Now, not only has he vengeance against the Dread Avenger on his mind, but all-out conquest–of Metro City, of the US and, ultimately, even the world! Can The Wraith stop this menace from destroying everything while battling the very citizens of his beloved city?

## COMING SOON!

### www.glowingeyesmedia.com

Books of Judgment Book One

# SANDERSON OF METRO

Frank Dirscherl & Bobby Nash

Two masters of the pulp fiction world, Frank Dirscherl and Bobby Nash, have come together to tell this tale, the secret NEVER before told origin of the first Wraith/Paul Sanderson, as only they could. This action-packed, atmospheric thrill could only be told now, and it could only be told by master storytellers like Dirscherl and Nash. An epic never to be repeated and not to be missed.

## NOW AVAILABLE!

**www.glowingeyesmedia.com**

## Books of Judgment Book Two
# SERPENT RISING
Frank Dirscherl & Greg Gick

The never-before-told origin story of The Wraith's arch nemesis the Cobra. Who he is, how he came to be, and how his and the original Paul Sanderson's life intertwined at key moments to cause them to become deadly adversaries. It's all here!

## NOW AVAILABLE!

### www.glowingeyesmedia.com

# About the Type

**Garamond** is a group of many old-style serif typefaces, originally those designed by Parisian craftsman Claude Garamond and other 16th century French engravers, and now many modern revivals. Though his name was written as 'Garamont' in his lifetime, the typefaces are generally spelled 'Garamond'. **Garamond Normal**, used in this book, is one of those modern revivals.

# Join FRANK DIRSCHERL and Glowing Eyes Media on social media!

facebook.com/glowingeyesmedia

@glowingeyesmedia

instagram.com/glowingeyesmedia

@glowingeyesmedia.bsky.social

glowingeyesmedia.proboards.com

All Glowing Eyes Media, The Wraith and Starflame novels, comics and merchandise can be obtained directly from the Glowing Eyes Media website – www.glowingeyesmedia.com

# Want to be The Wraith?

Well, it might be hard to actually *be* The Wraith, unless of course you, too, have been endowed with the power of the Eyes of Judgment. But you can certainly dress, drink and drive like him [*] (and you don't always have to be a millionaire to do so). See for yourselves.

The Wraith/Paul Sanderson wears:

- tailored clothing from Cad & the Dandy Tailors and Shirtmakers – www.cadandthedandy.co.uk
- bespoke footwear from Gaziano & Girling – www.gazianogirling.com
- watches from Héron (Marinor in Atlantic Blue) –

www.heronwatches.com/collections/marinor/products/marino r-atlantic-blue
- Armani Code cologne from Giorgio Armani – www.giorgioarmanibeauty-usa.com/for-him-armani-code/for-him-armani-code,default,sc.html

drinks:

- Twinings Earl & Lady Grey tea – www.twinings.co.uk
- Vittoria coffee – www.vittoriacoffee.com/

---

[*] Please note: Glowing Eyes Media does not condone drinking and driving. **All** adults, please always drink responsibly and **never** drink and drive

- The Balvenie Scotch whisky – www.thebalvenie.com
- Armand de Brignac champagne – www.armanddebrignac.com
- Cosmopolitan cocktails

uses:

- Dell laptops – www.dell.com.au
- Chesterfield furniture from Abbey Furniture
  www.chesterfieldfurnituremelbourne.com.au
- wallets from Launer - www.launer.com
- a Samsung Galaxy J5 Pro cell phone -
  www.samsung.com/latin_en/smartphones/galaxy-j5-2017/SM-
  J530GZDITPA/

drives:

- a Rolls Royce Wraith – www.rolls-roycemotorcars.com/en-
  GB/wraith.html

And, if you're really eager to actually look like The Wraith—in full costume—then you can always head over to Xtreme Design FX and let Lance Coulter there make you an exact replica of the costume used for The Wraith motion picture - www.xtremedesignfx.com

# HÉRON

Héron Marinor in Atlantic Blue - The Watch For Superheroes